FIMBULWINTER

A SKI SAGA

NATHAN ALEXANDER ROSS

FIMBULWINTER

A SKI SAGA

NATHAN ALEXANDER ROSS

ISBN (perfect): 978-19-15952-43-1
ISBN (hardcover): 978-19-15952-44-8
ISBN (epub): 978-19-15952-45-5

First printed Solstice, June 2025
by Sphinx (an imprint of Sul Books, LTD)
Lewes, UK / Rodenbourg, LUX
Cover and Interior Design: Sul Books
Cover image remixed by Sul Books and Nathan Alexander Ross

Find our books at SULBOOKS.COM

This one's for Rory. Thanks for showing me what mischief was.
And to Andrea. Thanks for your enduring patience.

How Quickly Things Change

Snow was falling heavily, a swirl of spiraling frost enveloping everything. Standing on the mountain, Lan's shaggy brown hair stuck out from under his helmet, freezing in the wind, as he stared into the blizzard.

He tried to watch singular flakes, but an intense vertigo hit him as he gazed into the clouds. It was all too much to take in — all of it blinding, all of it beautiful. He breathed happily. Everything made more sense in the chaos of a storm. He was strapped in, finally about to do what he'd been waiting months to do, to ski — or rather, snowboard — powder.

Snow was what Lan lived for, and women — but snow was simpler. Without snow, he had been overthinking things, wondering if he would ever do what his ex had told him to do and grow up already.

Breathe. Today is different. There was no snow the day before, and now there was two and a half feet. *Things can change so quickly. No more overthinking. Time to ski.*

As gravity began its slow pull upon him, drawing him down the mountain he called home, Lan let his body take over. He tried to calm his mind, to let the muscle memory return. *Remember,* he thought to himself. *Let your body sing.*

He said aloud, "I pray while I ski, for I am energy. We pray for snow so that we can flow; in that special place, where we let everything go."

His back leg swivelled and he felt bliss. The slope steepened; he floated along the powder. Lan leaned back and slid on his snowboard into oblivion. He found his line, bouncing out of bounds over downed trees, in and out of the closed signs, arriving at each turn with a confidence he lacked in the rest of his life.

This felt like what he was born to do. This was his magic, his body its vessel, extending into the environment around him, reading the landscape with senses beyond vision. Lan knew that powder skiing was the esoteric side of the sport, it was for those who wanted to get a *deeper* understanding of the mysteries of winter.

Pow was for breakfast and it was all he ever needed. But suddenly, his mind tried to take over, reminding him he was supposed to be working. He tried not to think, but then more thoughts came, this time that girl from the other day. *That one who prayed for snow*, he thought. *Wonder if it worked. Wonder if I'll see her again.*

He jumped off a lip, perhaps a little foolishly, and soared through the air. Upon landing, instead of finding bottomless glory, he heard, and felt, a terrible scrape as his board hit a jagged rock. He tomahawked into the snow with an awkward flip but then landed back on his feet and rode away laughing.

❧

At the same time, on top of a very important building very far away, a disgruntled man sat upon a rather large chair and yelled at his assistant.

"What kind of oracle is this?"

His assistant, a man with only one eye, grimaced as he looked down and away, diverting his gaze from the authoritative figure. He responded slowly.

"I did mention, sir, that you may not like what the oracle brings. To know the future is sometimes a curse...." He trailed off.

"The future? Ha!" Boomed the man in the chair. "Why are we coming back to this again? You still think this is the future? Despite all we have done to prevent it?"

"Respectably, sir, why do you ask about the prophecy if you never like what it predicts ... sir?"

"Silence!" The man on the throne yelled, his anger tinged with fear.

"I'm sorry, sir." His assistant continued to look at the ground.

"Well if this is all true." He paused with a sigh. "Hypothetically, it *can* still be changed, right?"

Silence.

"Can it not be changed?" he boomed.

"We have tried it before, but...." He was cut off.

"Do it again!" The manager screamed.

"Yes, sir."

The assistant said this aloud, but in his own head, with his own secret thoughts, he knew there was little hope. He himself had tried many times, but every action had led to the same destiny. Cut one root off, a new one grows in its place.

"Bring me the Fateweaver!" His boss yelled.

The man nodded and then kept his head lowered. *I must trust in his guidance,* he thought. *He is our only hope.* He then walked hurriedly away, a little confused, trying not to think too hard about the inevitable storm to come.

PART I: THE SOLSTICE

Linnea didn't know how she had made it to the top of the tram. She hadn't even thought it was open yet, but here she was. She then looked at the waffle in her hand, but it was gone. She didn't see her skis, or anyone else's, either. The only skis around were screwed into the building. Panic struck her — had she left them at the base?

She then noticed the smoke-filled sky, the sun barely visible through the haze. The mountains whose beauty awed her were mere hints of shadows through the thick smoke. There was no snow upon the glorious peaks, or even where she stood.

It's winter. There should be snow everywhere, especially up here.

"Excuse me." Linnea asked someone. "Where is all the snow? Why is no one skiing? It's the middle of winter!"

A man whose facial features were blurry like an unfocused photograph responded. "Ha! It doesn't snow here anymore. People haven't skied here for years...."

Linnea's heart began to beat quickly as fear gripped her. It was so hot up here! The trees she could see had turned a reddish-brown; no birds fluttered about. She looked down to the valley: the river! Her precious river, it was nowhere to be seen, merely a dry pit of sand, snaking through the valley. She would never boat again! Fires burned, smoldering in the valley.

She began running around the top of the mountain in tears, then tripped. It felt like she fell into a hole. Darkness surrounded her. As images appeared, she realized she was in the middle of a great battle. Beings too large to comprehend filled the sky, their feet crashing down all around. She dropped to the ground, and then looked up.

A group of massive figures — giants? — were huddled around two lumps. Linnea saw that they were grieving, and noticed what they were looking at. Two bodies lay dying upon the ground. One had an aura of ice and snow. The other was radiating green.

Linnea then woke in a sweat, jumping up off her pillow, unsure what had happened in her dream. All she knew was that it was a terrible vision, atrocious and dark. It was a nightmare, but something else had clicked inside of her; like she had discovered something in that forgotten dream, something like her true purpose, her true will. She pulled herself out of bed, walked her dog in the sunshine, and got ready to go skiing, hoping it would snow today, hoping her terrible dream would never come true.

Although currently, it didn't feel far off. There was no snow.

Lan looked out from the lift over the sad ski run known as the "strip of death." Snow-making allowed for some pitiful skiing in early December, but it was better than none. No snow in Colorado, California still hadn't stopped burning, and Teton Hole, Wydaho, had never seen so little moisture.

He tried to listen to the people he shared the chair with. They held their phones up close to their faces, blocking the sun, staring at their glowing screens.

"Yah ... no ... no snow in the forecast. Too warm ...."

Lan laughed to himself. Typical small talk. Awkward silence? How about the weather? Of course, ask about the weather and people always pull their phones out to confirm what they're seeing right in front of them.

Lan had never made the transition: he still had a flip phone. He didn't trust screens. Sometime after high school, as he realized how absurd his dreams of becoming a secret agent were, he was amazed at how brainwashed he had become. So, he began to question his relationship with television and its alluring glow. The screen seemed to hypnotize him, almost *possess* him, for hours on end. And when smartphones became more popular, he didn't trust those screens, either.

This didn't happen overnight though. In his avoidance of the television, Lan became a photographer, getting out into the mountains and recreating. The internet seemed a little less mind-controlling than TV at first, and Lan was a part of the first generation to have social media. But social media soon started to feel just as toxic.

He noticed that while he was out in some breathtaking location taking a photo, his mind was already on the internet, thinking about what he would say about the shot as if his identity was now on the line. Once again, he felt *possessed*. And it seemed like others were, too.

As the faces of the other people on the lift absorbed into their phones, Lan looked around, trying to be attentive. But the lack of snow was depressing, and his thoughts turned dark.

He was too afraid to think the unthinkable, yet too cynical to deny it. The last few winters had been unpredictable and the west was dry. Lan didn't need science to know the climate was changing — he could feel it. It was obvious how badly humans had been treating the planet. And if it stopped snowing regularly, there would be no snowpack. No snowpack meant no rivers, and no rivers meant no fresh water.

The repercussions were terrifying — especially *no snow*. Lan had become a ski bum purely for the snow and shaped his entire life around it. He loved snow more than anything, and he was over the idea that voting could save snow, or that voting could fix anything. Lan knew drastic changes needed to happen, but he wasn't really sure what to do. The problems seemed too gigantic.

Another skier on the lift interrupted Lan's thoughts. "I miss the good old days when Teton Hole had tons of snow in December." But when no one responded, the older skier went back to scrolling.

Lan looked up at the sky: a few dark clouds had formed over the mountains. The internet said it would be sunny all day. The sky ahead proved different — it even felt suddenly colder.

A memory swelled in Lan's gut. Growing up, climbing mountains with his family: whenever the weather was turning sour, his mom had always asked the mountain gods for help, asking the storm to leave. But now, Lan wanted the weather to be sour: he wanted a storm.

"How about we say a little prayer for snow?" Lan said aloud.

The others seemed surprised by this sudden outburst. But then, so was Lan. He wasn't exactly religious. When he was in church as a kid, he would daydream of bad guys bursting through the church windows with guns. Lan would then imagine himself fighting them off to save the day. The screen had obviously hijacked his imagination.

At first, the Bible had just seemed like a story some old people had made up. But as Lan got older, and his dad got him more into mythology, he realized how story and imagination were everything. Maybe there was more to this religion thing, maybe these old people had experienced something real ... even if it didn't make rational sense.

Lan didn't believe in "capital G" god, but he suspected the world was full of other gods. He had come across the trickster myth, one of the oldest stories humans have. It fit with his own paradoxical view of the world. The trickster seemed like proof that spirituality wasn't all Jesus and his angry dad. It could also be mischief and revelry, an artistic rebellion that causes cosmic revolution.

So, why not pray for snow as some sort of skid mysticism?

A girl sitting on the far side of the lift suddenly asked, "A prayer to whom?"

"The mountain gods, of course!" Lan replied, laughing, happy someone had engaged.

"Ok, I'll lead it," she said, without hesitation. "Dear mountainous spirits of lore, we ask you to bless our sad little western town with the snow it so dearly deserves. Come to us in our time of need to make the people, mountains, and animals thrive. We pray for snow so that life can continue to grow."

As she finished her prayer, just as they neared the top of the chairlift, a gust of wind blasted their faces, whirling out of the void; swaying the chair strongly. The sun found its way through the clouds and hit the blowing snow, giving Lan a glimpse of a rainbow of color reflecting off the swirling wind.

"A-fucking-men!" Lan hollered, laughing. "Praise the mountain gods!" He then slid off the lift.

He looked at the girl. She was cute, and she was smiling. She glanced at him briefly, lifted her head in a nod, and skied off down the hill.

Lan still had to strap into his snowboard, so he lost sight of her in the crowd. *Dammit,* he thought. *Why does everyone look the same in winter?* He bombed the strip of death looking for her as the clouds hid the sun. With only one run open, there were too many people in the small space.

He lost her. He lost the girl who prayed for snow.

An hour later, it was snowing.

Later that night, Lan wrote his own little prayer poem in his journal. He was skeptical, but he also felt desperate, desperate enough to pray. The phones had said it wouldn't snow, but the skies outside proved different. *Maybe there is something to this prayer thing,* he mused.

He read aloud the words he wrote. "I pray while I ski, for I am energy. We pray for snow so that we can flow; in that special place, where we let everything go."

Linnea barely made it to work on time. She put her hair up, then realized she maybe should have showered. She took off her shirt and washed her armpits in the sink as fast as she could. She poured some essential oil on her hands, rubbed it on as much of her skin as she could, and then took a deep breath.

It had finally started snowing that afternoon while she was skiing, so it had been difficult for her to stop. A couple of inches fell within an hour, and skiing in the fresh fluff made her forget about time. She couldn't stop smiling through the heavy falling flakes, skiing into lost and found happiness. The snow had arrived, and it warmed her soul, but she'd almost forgotten she had to go to work.

Linnea walked out of the kitchen to see how many people were in the restaurant. Empty. Her smile persisted. The holiday rush hadn't come yet. Early December was already the least busy time of the season, and since there was no snow, no one was in town.

Linnea dreaded the tourists, despite needing their money. Her off-season had been amazing, but she'd spent much more money than she meant to. Being in the service industry involved a love/hate relationship with the tourist industry. You need the tourists but don't like the crowds and traffic they create.

Sometimes Linnea wondered what this town would look like if it wasn't entirely reliant on tourism, but that was the kind of question you weren't supposed to ask. *Two more weeks of calm,* she thought. *Enjoy it while it's here.* Christmas break meant madness and money.

Right then, a family of four walked in.

The family sat in Linnea's section. She served them water and introduced herself. Although they were quite dressed up, they didn't have much to say, and only the mother spoke to Linnea. The father and two boys barely even talked to each other: they had their phones out the whole time.

When the family had finished eating and were about to settle their bill, the woman, whose diamond earrings and massive ring suddenly stuck out to Linnea, asked Linnea a baffling question.

"Excuse me, miss. I hope you don't mind me asking, but do you go to church?"

Linnea didn't know what to say. Customers say some weird things, but this was a new one. Then, she thought about how she had prayed for snow earlier that day and figured that would suffice.

"Well, actually, earlier I said a little prayer to the mountain gods, I prayed for snow, and look!" She motioned outside. "Now it's snowing!"

The mother laughed sarcastically. The father glanced up from his phone with a chuckle.

"Oh, honey, that's nice, but we're not heathens who pray to false gods. We mean, have you accepted Jesus Christ as your lord and savior? This is all God's creation, you see, and you seem like a nice young lady, we just wanted to invite you to a little service at our church tomorrow."

The woman handed her a pamphlet.

These people live in town? Linnea was shocked. She didn't know anyone who went to church. *Who does she think she is calling me a heathen?*

"Oh thanks, well ... yeah, let me know when it is, maybe I'll come." She felt guilty for lying, slipped the pamphlet into her pocket, and glanced at the other members of the family. The two children were teenagers; neither looked up at her, lost as they were in their screens. The husband was still on his phone as well but glanced at Linnea with a weird smirk.

"Y'know, it's funny you say you prayed for snow," the woman said almost ironically, "a few members of our church run a non-profit that fights to reduce carbon emissions in Teton Hole, we donate regularly." The woman said this with a self-satisfied smile.

"Oh, that's cool!" Linnea was surprised to hear this.

"The service is at nine o'clock, you should invite some friends because we would love to see more young adults at the church."

Linnea walked from the table, feeling a little thrown off. She had never really felt like Christianity promoted caring about nature — had it changed? She glanced down at the check with disappointment and back at the slightly older woman, wearing her fancy dress, trying to engage her family. *Donates regularly but only tips ten percent?*

Linnea sighed and pulled her own phone out.

The weather forecast had changed drastically since earlier that day — now it was supposed to snow all week! She looked outside: it was still dumping. Maybe this prayer had worked after all? No Jesus required. She glanced back at her phone and began scrolling.

National Geographic had posted a picture of a snake. She stared at it briefly, its curves reminding her of fresh ski tracks, and then remembered the snake from the Bible. That was the main thing she didn't like about church: the way they spun women to be the cause of the fall from paradise. Eve was the original sinner, the cause of all of humanity's problems. Linnea didn't think people had been cast from paradise. It was right here, on earth.

She laughed and said to herself, "I'm not going inside to get to church tomorrow, I'm going skiing. In Paradise. I doubt Jesus will be there, but I will find some sort of magical spirits."

Linna laughed to herself again. It was kind of funny the woman had called her a heathen: Linnea's main aspiration recently had been to become a bit of a witch. She and her roommate had been talking a lot about the witch hunts of medieval times, and how women used to be the doctors and healers in society, but by accusing women of witchcraft, they were easily removed from their higher status.

She and her roommate had been pulling Tarot cards, and reading about magic, astrology, and energy. She doubted they would be into that at church. She then looked back at her phone.

The snake in the photo seemed to stare out of the screen, into her soul.

Lan got off the bus in the dark, hiding his beer from the bus driver. He was pooped — literally. Most people think that when you move to a ski town, you are probably going to end up being a ski instructor, or a lifty, or a server who skis all day and works at night.

Instead, Lan's job was to deal with human waste. Today's work involved having to remove a toilet from a wall because the clog wouldn't go away. That clog had flooded the bathroom with toilet paper and fecal bits.

Thankfully, today's skiing was incredible, and the snow cleaned the mess off his snow pants with ease. The cliff-hucking had officially begun — within reason, of course — so Lan was happy. Poo was normal. He was used to it. He should probably get paid more, but he could tolerate it as long as it kept snowing, which it currently did.

Pierce, his roommate texted. "You almost home? We have to talk."

Pierce was actually his roommate, coworker, and best friend. This much time together wasn't always easy, but luckily they had a bit of a bromance which somehow continued through the chaos of the seasons.

Lan didn't text back. He would be home soon anyway, and Pierce probably just wanted to get a drink. Lan joked that he often "Pierce Pressured" him into drinking. Lan was also maybe easily convinced.

He rolled a cigarette and crunched his way down the street, actively looking for patches of ice to break, enjoying the sound and feeling of ice crackling under his boots. Snow fluttered by like butterflies, swirling in the street lights. He felt euphoric and grateful.

Music bumped from the house as Lan walked through his yard. Someone had made a snowman, giving it lopsided breasts and a carrot wiener. As he walked through the yard, a raven cawed at him from the roof of the Brown House.

He instantly got chills. Ravens were tricksters, and he had been seeing them everywhere. He stared at it for a minute in awe. It continued to screech at him, silhouetted above the Brown House, yelling messages he couldn't understand. *Maybe it's about my house?*

The Brown House was a classic skid house, full of freaks and the sorts of troublemakers who mostly just make trouble for themselves. Their downward economic mobility aligned well with their downward mobility on the ski slopes.

He laughed as he walked in because an eruption of noise filled his ears. People hollered over the music at his arrival. A crowd of ski bums sat in his living room, passing around a spliff.

"Lan-slide!" "Lan-fill!" "Lantern!" Lan had to step over a snowboard, four empty beer cans, and an array of boots to make his way to them.

Lan had lived here for the last five years. Though other roommates came and went, he and Pierce stuck it out even as $350 rent each had become $550, and then suddenly $850. Everyone else's rent in town was even higher, but the Brown House was old and worn down, so the landlord couldn't charge as much, even with the housing crisis.

The ski town had a billionaire problem. It wasn't that there was nowhere to live, but that there was nowhere to build: all the property was already owned. No income tax — and tons of wild and protected, breathtaking land — meant a lot of rich people bought property there. Of course, they only lived here for maybe one month of the year. While most of Lan's friends had moved six or seven times in five years or moved away entirely, most of the mansions sat empty.

If there was Feng Shui to the Brown House, it consisted of beer, pizza, and old skis. The walls were plastered with posters that looked like they hadn't been moved since the eighties. The living room had three couches, none of whose cushions offered any back support. A broken lava lamp sat beside the dirty bong; the clutter was impressive.

A man with a rather unkempt beard — their newest "roommate" — handed Lan the spliff. Of course, his "room" was the living room and he slept on the couch. Everyone called him "Couch Guy," and called his dog "Couch Dog."

"Dude, remind me later to tell you about this crazy stuff I was reading," he said to Lan.

Couch Guy was Lan's old buddy from college. He had showed up with an RV full of ganja this last summer and never left. Weed is still illegal in Wydaho, so he had plenty of clientele. His RV, which he called "the Naughty Cowgirl," sat on the driveway, and that's where he slept all summer. Now that winter set in and it was cold, he kind of … well, moved inside.

Couch Guy didn't pay rent, but he sometimes paid utilities. Lan didn't mind him being around because he loved talking to him about random philosophical shit, but Pierce wasn't so sure about him. Couch Guy was probably the main reason for tension between Lan and Pierce.

"Where is Pierce?" Lan asked the Couch Guy.

He motioned towards the bathroom. "In there, bro. Can't you hear him?"

Lan listened, then heard Pierce cursing above the din of the music.

"You need a hand in there? Are you dying?" Lan yelled.

"Dude this damn toilet is clogged again!" Pierce opened the door, and Lan walked over, feeling like his life revolved around going from one toilet to another. Then he saw how much toilet paper was in the toilet.

"Looks like someone needs a lesson in folding toilet paper," he said to Pierce. "Don't we deal with this enough at work?"

Pierce looked guilty and put his hands up. "What do you mean — you fold your toilet paper?"

"Uh, yeah...." Lan said, slowly.

Genuinely surprised, Pierce continued. "I kinda just bunch it up into a little ball." Everyone in the living room then erupted in laughter.

"Dude, I stopped doing that when I was like five years old," Lan said.

"Whatever, I'm changing the subject, ok? Lan, you have to see this BS."

He then handed Lan a piece of paper. "We're being evicted. This was taped to the door. And get this, the notice says we were 'distributing the peace,' not disturbing the peace."

Everyone but Lan laughed.

"That can't be serious!" Lan said, shaking his head.

"Dead serious," Pierce replied. "It says we gotta be out at the end of the month."

Lan didn't believe it. He and the Couch Guy stared in disbelief at the piece of paper. It looked fairly official, even if it did say they were being evicted for distributing the peace.

"That can't be real." Couch Guy said, his eyes glazed over. "This is in no way a legal document."

"How do *you* know?" Pierce asked, finding another reason to be annoyed with him.

"I went to law school for a semester, dude." Couch Guy said this quite seriously, but everyone laughed anyway.

Lan was reeling. Something was up with this typo. It was too weird. After a moment, he said, "I'm telling you, this house has a spirit to it, a trickster spirit. It has been around for, I dunno, how long? Had skids living in it for like forty years? It has something to do with this typo, it doesn't want us kicked out. As the notice says: we merely 'distribute peace.'"

Couch Guy chimed in. "I mean yeah, I sell weed, what is more peaceful than that?"

"Shove it, Couch Guy!" Pierce said angrily. "It's probably your goddamn RV that is the cause of this, you know, that one you don't even sleep in?"

Lan shrugged. "Who does this landlord even think he is? Doesn't he know this land can't *really* be owned? It is all stolen land."

"Oh, come off it. F'ing Lan, always talking about stolen land. This is serious." Pierce said.

"Well, what are we going to do about it?" Lan asked.

"I'll call the landlord tomorrow," Pierce replied.

"Pierce pressure him out of it, bro." Lan said, refusing to accept what this news really meant.

Whoever was in charge of the sky seemed to set it into slow motion. Rain is often chaotic and generally a bit unpleasant; snow, on the other hand, is frequently relaxing. Happy petals of fluffy ice floated down majestically, drifting into Linnea's mind with a beauty she found spiritual as if the frosty water somehow rearranged time.

And if watching the snow fall wasn't already a spiritual experience in itself, moving across it on skis enhanced it; it felt like the interplay between snow and ski somehow connected her to divinity. Her body mingled with the snow, a dance, the motion a key part of the union and, although thoughts occasionally helped with the next decision, the body appeared to have its own language. The mind could hardly keep up, it merely translated the landscape into rhythm and kept the focus going. Each movement was choreographed to the music of the mountains, every minuscule shift reflecting the beauty before her.

So much snow — Linnea could hardly believe it. Her prayer had worked!

She had decided to still refer to it as a prayer. After that woman had called her a heathen, she had wondered: do heathens pray? Prayer felt kind of, well, Christian. Recently, she was trying to distance herself from monotheistic frameworks, to instead work and play within, for lack of a better term, pagan frameworks. She was currently grateful for this because the woman had been a bit offensive.

As the snow flew up and hit her in the face, she spoke to the trees around her with glee.

"Call me heathen," she said aloud. "I refuse to be offended."

Since high school, she had slightly rejected her Christian upbringing and simplified whatever her religious feelings were into "worshipping nature." But with research and time; she came to realize this was nothing new. There was a history behind worshipping nature, and it was actually a bit dark. She learned there are all kinds of "pagan religions," because the term essentially applied to anyone who isn't Christian. Many worshipped deities connected to the land they lived on. Of course, most of these people were basically erased from Western culture — to put it nicely. This culminated with the Roman conversion, the Dark Ages, the witch hunts, the invasion of the New World, and globalization in general. Many pagan traditions continued in the background but they were hidden.

Linnea hadn't really been the one to call it a "prayer for snow." That was the random guy on the lift, but she went all in because you rarely get anyone praying for anything nowadays.

She had considered calling the prayer for snow a "spell" for snow, but it didn't quite have the same ring. She then decided Christians shouldn't have a monopoly on prayer. Maybe the speaking aloud part was the key to the thought manifesting in the universe — the vibration of the voice being medicine for the wind.

But, Linnea wondered, what is the difference between a prayer and a spell? An offering or an oath? Does it really matter? The intention seemed the most important part. Maybe prayer was a radical response to life's circumstances; a form of action, not merely wishful thinking.

All this thinking about prayer had caused Linnea to look at the pamphlet the woman had given her the other night inviting her to church, but it didn't exactly resonate. She had recently read about "re-wilding" Christianity. She liked the idea — maybe Christianity is more nature-based now that it used to be — but when all you care about is your spirit getting to heaven, you tend to forget where you come from.

Something about European pre-Christian peoples had really fascinated her. She was reading endless books on the subject, feeling like her ancestors had lived lives much more connected to the natural world, much more respectful of the earth. She knew better than to overly-romanticize the past, but she appreciated the pre-Christian connection to spirit *and* body.

But really, Linnea was here for the divinity of the body, the movement and dancing, as well as the psychic and supernatural. Her body bounced back and forth, through the forest, over the bumps, and under the branches; her legs screaming the whole way. She was not in shape yet, but she was connecting with the land, and that was the part that mattered.

Skiing seemed to her a sacred dance that helps us worship nature and all the material and spiritual complexity it entails. As she glided down the mountain through the miraculous snow, she felt grateful to be taking part in a history which had been obscured, embracing a feminine need to dance and thanking the snow the whole time. She felt the mountain gods with her.

It felt wild to Lan how much his emotional state could change so quickly. One week, there is no snow and everything sucks. The next, it dumps four feet and everything is awesome. Then, suddenly you are being evicted and everything sucks again. Of course, then you get very drunk, but that's only a temporary escape.

This eviction was real, he was on the brink of a full-on existential crisis, and his hangover didn't help.

Lan slogged back into the Cave after morning shovel rounds, feeling apathetic. The Cave was their work "office," but it was really just an old garage decorated with random ski signs and a haphazard clutter of tools and shovels all located right next to the dumpster and recycling area.

"That sucks about your eviction, man. Why don't you just buy a house?" Lan's boss asked as they sat down. "It was the best decision I ever made."

"Buy a house?" Lan asked, incredulously. "How in the hell will I do that? You bought way before the property values exploded. Even if for some reason they gave me a loan for the eight hundred thousand dollars a house would cost, I would be paying that off the rest of my damn life."

"Well," his boss said. "You know what my dad used to tell me? You can't be a pussy your whole life."

Lan had heard this already from him. "Yeah, yeah. But also, how about you give me a fucking raise?"

"It's not my call, Lan. I would if it were. But this place isn't a democracy." He smirked.

"Too true." Lan laughed.

Lan had grown up in the suburbs and then had run off to a small town to get away from everything. He then learned that you can never really get away from society — you just get a little more rural. Even in small towns, all the same rules apply to money. You need it, and it runs all the politics — especially in a town run by billionaires.

Lan's boss, on the other hand, was one of those people who seemed to do the small-town thing well. Sure, Lan was "making it work," but he was years away from ever owning land, at least around here. He also wasn't sure you could ever actually own land. You can't own a person, so why can you own a specific place?

It didn't help that Lan was poor. He had fully embraced the metaphor of downward mobility in both skiing and in life, hoping to somehow make up for some of the privilege he had had. Anyway, the future seemed dumb. Or maybe he was. He was now considering leaving town more than he ever had. How long had he been living this lifestyle? Being an under-glorified snow shoveling custodial handyman? Maybe too long.

The eviction seemed like a sign to jump ship, to travel the world, to work for a non-profit, and to help people. Maybe it was time to finally live up to his ideals and fight for indigenous reconciliation? To actually do something with his life? He loved the people in this community, but half the time he hung out with them he ended up drunk. Sure the people were fit, but they also drank — *a lot.*

He sighed as his boss handed him a beer.

"This will help, bud," he said with a wink.

Lan laughed. At least it is some sort of community ... more than some people can say.

Breathe, he told himself. *It's just this damn eviction that has got me down.*

His boss continued. "But seriously, get over yourself, we have work to do."

"I have been shoveling all morning!" Lan said in response. "More than you can say, you just got here."

His boss winked at him again.

Fifteen minutes later, Lan was laughing to himself as he crushed the beer can and got off the gondola. Life wasn't so bad, he would work more soon. In the meantime: he had other priorities.

Suddenly everything felt fine again because he started skiing, and the movement allowed those frustrated emotions to just slip away. He looked out at the mountains and thought, *mountains are home.* He glanced at Grand Teton, and its glory bathed him in awe. It seemed a vortex, a sacred place, somewhere that deserved to be respected. Maybe he should stay, help spread that sacred awe, and finally write that damn book he had been talking about for years. He and Pierce would find a new place to live, and who knows? Lan might just find a girl to hang out with. And maybe she would want to be poor with him.

Tourists were already starting to arrive and with them mixed feelings for Linnea. December was always the slowest part of the season until about the eighteenth; then, suddenly, people started showing up *en masse*. With the holidays just around the corner, people were out to spend some money. Linnea was out to bank off that — most of the town was. It was the first big rush.

Linnea was on the verge of being annoyed after an extremely busy night, but she had made some good money. Most of her annoyance came from her last table, a group of dudes who would have been attractive individually but were complete dicks together.

Why are all the guys around here such bros? Linnea wondered. None of them seemed to want girlfriends — they won't talk to you in person, but then hit you up online when they want sex. It seemed all the best guys were already taken.

The other thing that annoyed her was the current state of her body — tired from skiing and still recovering from drinking two nights before. Well, and a little drinking yesterday, and a few beers while skiing today. She hadn't been eating well either, her winter goals were already proving to be a giant failure.

She wasn't proud of it, but in the last two weeks, drinking seemed the only way to get her body back to some happy state after work. *Dear god,* she thought — *happy state? Is it really a happy state? Or just some socially accepted feedback loop of separation? Making us forget our bodies for a time until we are brutally reminded that we have them, or that we* are *them?*

She was in that situation again, getting off work and craving a glass of wine. Just one, really, but she knew it would be more.

"No," she said to herself. "This alcohol feedback loop has got to end. Time to recenter." She reminded herself that the alcohol sections in the stores are referred to as "spirits" for a reason. They can take over your body, *possess* you.

She decided to go home and get some rest. Maybe she would see if Sylvia or Boots wanted to do yoga tomorrow. Or maybe she should just be alone, slow down, and have some time with herself and her dog.

She went home, walked Bailey, and hung out with her roommate Sylvia for a bit. They made plans to do yoga the next day, which made her feel better about everything, so she went right to bed. Rest would also help.

She snuggled Bailey and tried to read a few pages in her book. She couldn't really focus, so she turned on a show, and then let the screen distract her mind until her eyelids felt heavy. She finally switched the television off and found sand at the bottom of her dreams that turned into snow. She was skiing powder, but it felt all broken up like she kept teleporting to different parts of the mountain. The flow wasn't there.

Her dream then became even weirder. An ominous feeling swept through her. She was in the thick of a forest, watching a massive wolf move through the trees. It stopped and then stared back at her. The wolf's fur was pitch black, and its deep yellow eyes were somehow like the sun. She felt mildly terrified because those fiery globes seemed to stare right into her. She felt cold. Still, the wolf was beautiful. She tried to ski towards it, but then the snow fell heavier, and she drifted into new dreams.

The next morning, Linnea got some juice at the juice bar with Sylvia, her roommate. They walked through the cold air, kicking the fresh snow, talking about wolves and dreams. Linnea had only ever seen one wolf in her life — on a trip to Yellowstone two years ago. It had been the most beautiful creature she had ever seen.

"Wolves are my favorite animal," Sylvia said.

There was a huge debate around here about wolves. The ranchers didn't like them, they often ate livestock, but their re-introduction had literally transformed the ecosystem.

The screen of her mind kept revisiting that wolf staring at her as they walked into the yoga studio. It felt too vivid. She told Sylvia about it. "Have you ever had a dream that felt so real, it makes you tingle all over when you recall it?"

"Those are the best dreams!" Sylvia said. "Thank you for sharing. Maybe it's a sign, maybe you *will* see that wolf."

Linnea wanted to talk more, but they had arrived. She was avoiding bringing something up. She was nervous about this date she had agreed to go on with this guy. He seemed nice, though she wasn't sure if she was into it. She felt obligated to go — he had sent her a nice message online and then approached her in person — but she barely knew him.

She began thinking about how she was over the men in this town but then stopped herself. *Stop thinking,* she thought. *You're doing yoga.*

She told herself to breathe and relax. *Be conscious of your body, it's not hungover anymore, it feels good.*

She breathed deeply and stretched, letting oxygen seep into stagnant muscles. She told herself to find peace and silence through the breathing, the being. *Your body is a temple,* she thought again. *Treat it as such. Worship it. And look for the wolf inside. Maybe it is your spirit animal.*

Elsewhere, dark clouds loomed over another layer of polluted air. Towering peaks pierced the cold horizon, snowy mountains surrounded a twinkling city.

A large man, his long hair and beard both a dirty blond, stood upon a peak and looked down at the lights, fearful of what he was about to do. He gazed through cold, old eyes, though he felt in himself the energy of a young man.

He was here again, a place he had left long ago. He stared at the old city at the base of the mountains in fearful contemplation. In the middle of the city sat an ancient castle, jutting upwards. But it was ringed by modern skyscrapers and, beyond them, a sprawl of unremarkable houses. Fumes filled the skies.

He shuddered at the sight. This was why he was here. Things were going to change. His old wooden skis already bound upon his feet, he prepared to descend into that ancient, holy city.

He saw his line. Time to ski. Time to let go, time to discover his fate. He cut left across the glowing snow, headed for the spine, but then suddenly saw an opportunity to jump. He did and was airborne and free.

When he landed, he sank down to the depths and praised the holiness of this, his favorite substance. Cutting back right, he rode the glorious spine, taking turns on each edge, the draconic ridge of fresh snow crumbling below him. His speed gained, so he checked it with a slash before one more huck and then continued down towards the sparkling city. Few would dare to take this route.

He never liked prophecies or wanted to believe them. The problem with prophecies, he had thought, is the people who don't want the prophecy to come true. They do everything in their power to stop them from happening, while the ones supposed to help make it happen usually haven't even heard them.

He had, fortunately, been informed. And he was taking action, helping to make it happen. But he wasn't doing this for the prophecy itself. Instead, something very old had awoken inside of him. He had changed. He was in love, and he was doing this all for love.

Others had called him a ski bum, and maybe this was true. A ski bum doesn't desire much and doesn't require much. Just one thing, one much bigger than them: snow. If snow is the goddess to a ski bum, and that goddess had a knife to her throat, what would that ski bum do? He would have to fight for her, fight for winter, fight for snow.

It was late, but he didn't need to go much farther. There was no denying his nervousness, but he had been assured multiple times that he would have no trouble; the guards would already be dealt with. He felt fortunate to have allies right now.

The rest of the city lay quietly in their beds as he approached the building. As promised, the door was unprotected. He entered the access code provided to him and the door slid open seamlessly.

The large man walked down the long hallway towards another door. He jumped slightly when he noticed something on the ground. It was a guard, but it wasn't moving; it had been drugged. The second door opened mechanically.

He moved slowly at first, gazing in fear at the object upon the stand. His heart raced as he approached it. How could something so small be of such importance?

There was no time to question. He grabbed the ancient artifact and fled. No going back now. He was committed. *There is no courage without fear.*

9: Coyote Tricks

Lan drove north in his run-down Subaru whose spoiler was a rusty old bike rack. He rubbed his bloodshot eyes, scratched his beard, and gazed at the mountains looming to the west. The peaks of the Tetons were enveloped in clouds, while small snowflakes fell in the valley.

Lan kept his eyes trained on the land before him. He was looking for animals to photograph with his DSLR camera and its telephoto lens. Antlers from a herd of elk speckled the landscape, and Lan watched them in awe.

He had skied all morning, but after a couple of hikes to ski some untouched powder, he decided to leave a little early. Pierce had been trying to get him to drink, but he didn't want to drink too much to-day. The season had barely begun, and he needed to pace himself.

His house had become a constant party since the news of the eviction — their way of fighting a war that can't be won was to ignore it. Pierce knew so many people in town and assured Lan that something would work out soon. But Lan was panicked about it and skeptical that Pierce would come through.

Getting out into nature certainly helped bring clarity to his thoughts. Just looking at the Tetons seemed to calm his anxiety. But still, Lan couldn't stop thinking about the eviction or about landlords. He'd read recently about the Enclosures in Europe, that moment when they started putting up fences and telling people the land they used was suddenly not theirs any longer. And that's where landlords came from, "lords of the land."

Those landlords stole land in Europe and then came to the Americas to steal it from the natives. This all put his current landlord situation in perspective. The billionaires had flooded the market of this place, and no one else had any chance. The billionaires influenced all the politics as well. They knew that affordable housing would bring "too many" poor people to town, and they didn't want poor people in town.

Billionaires owned all the land the government didn't, and they protected their image by supporting their own version of conservation. They didn't actually care about the people in town, just the pristine vision of pure, untouched nature. Meanwhile, the Latinos who worked for them were all jammed together, two families at a time, into small motel rooms.

Suddenly, a raven flew right above Lan's car, pulling him from his thoughts. It felt like a reminder to pay attention. He was, after all, there to look for animals.

Lan turned a corner and then slammed on his brakes. There, in the middle of the road, was a massive bison, as big as Lan's tiny car. Lan pulled out his camera and snapped a few shots, surprised to find a buffalo this far south. Its size awed him, and he felt grateful. So few of these creatures who once covered the continent were left, and Lan was fortunate to live in one of the only places they still roamed free.

"Thank you, mighty bison, for blessing me with your awesome presence." He said this aloud and then looked back at the mountains.

Teewinot stuck out from the clouds like a mysterious canine tooth. He had been on top of it a few times — it was one of his favorites. He'd been trying to be more appreciative of these natural places; to not think of climbing a mountain as conquering it like so many others did. He also didn't want to be thinking about what he would say on social media as he took a photo of a beautiful animal. He wanted to show his appreciation of these powerful forces, not turn them into victims or commodities. They aren't here merely for our consumption.

The main thing about this current mindset, enforced by the billionaires, was that nature was not a place that was meant to have humans in it unless they were tourists. He thought to himself darkly, *this is why there are no Native Americans in the national parks.*

But humans are a part of nature, Lan reasoned. We just have to shift our perspective of dominating and conquering it to something more relationship-based. A give-back relationship. Lan's own hypocrisy was what spurred him to consider alternatives: a ski resort doesn't exactly care about the land it is on, although they claim they do. "We are Green, we buy shares in wind power!" they say.

Lan had been driving again as he thought about all this. He tried to force his mind back to focus on what he was there for. *You're looking for animals*, he scolded himself. *Keep your stoned eyes looking!*

As Lan approached a crossroads something moved in the bushes near him. He reached for his camera and tried to stop quietly, but his brakes squeaked anyway. Still, the figure in the bushes — like a dog — was there. Lan hoped it was a wolf, but then he saw the fierce gold-brown eyes fixed on him. It was just fifteen feet away: a coyote.

Lan pulled his camera up to his eye and used its lens to look closer at the coyote's face. Rugged lines of frosty hair rippled around its snout, speckled with a confetti of snow.

He took a shot, and then another. Click, click, click. Still, the coyote seemed unfazed. It even came closer, too close now for Lan's giant lens.

He put the camera down.

Lan and the coyote stared at each other for what felt like an eternity. He had read that coyotes were tricksters in Native American mythology, and while gazing into those eyes he felt something stir in him. Maybe it was some sort of ancient wisdom, something he couldn't quite put words to. Lan laughed quietly, amused and amazed at this inter-species staring contest. The coyote seemed like a steward of the land, testing Lan to see if he was worthy to be here.

Lan shuddered. A car started to drive down the road towards them. He glanced towards it and when he looked back the coyote was gone. Not even a rustle in the bushes. Just — gone.

The unnatural music was shaking the rickety old house. Just as Linnea walked into the party, her eyeballs were blasted by vibrant colors — a multitude of ragged old Christmas sweaters filled with humans packed the living room. Half the crowd moved their limbs wildly to the sounds being projected by a man at a DJ booth, while the other half of the room yelled about face shots. People were taking turns doing shot-skis, while a game of beer pong was happening on a tiny table.

This was ski culture. Thirty DJs, two bands. Linnea sighed, and then wondered, *where the heck is Chelsea?* And then: *why the hell am I even here?*

She made her way through the chaos towards the back of the room and found Chelsea chatting away out on the deck. Linnea, about to turn around and head out, felt a light tap on her shoulder. It was Jack, the guy she had gone on a date with the other night — whose texts she had been ignoring since then.

The date was not her favorite. Jack was a ski instructor and didn't stop talking about himself for the first half of the evening. And then, mid-date, as some clients randomly walked by, he invited them to sit down with them. The sweater he wore tonight was cheesy, with words declaring something about an old-fashioned family Christmas while blinking with cheap lights.

Linnea said a quick "Oh, hey," but then Jack went in for a hug and she started to step back. Thankfully, just then, Chelsea burst through the door, shouting, and interrupting him with her body.

"Nea!"

Linnea swooped towards Chelsea, dancing with joy, hugging her instead, leaving Jack looking sad, twinkling awkwardly in his ugly sweater.

"Linnea, where did you get that sweater? You look like a festive babe!" Chelsea exclaimed.

Linnea blushed slightly and looked down at her sweater. Its red, green, and blue colors were a psychedelic swirl of spirals with snowflakes patterned across it. It fit tight, accentuating her curves. Chelsea, on the other hand, had the largest sweater Linnea had ever seen. It hung down to her knees and looked almost like a dress. There were a few elves stitched into it drunkenly holding beers with the words, "Let's get Elfed Up!" written below.

Chelsea was Linnea's favorite person to ski with and also one of her favorite people in general. Chelsea was beyond eccentric, always making all kinds of weird high-pitched noises, cracking jokes, and having more fun than anyone else around. She helped Linnea just laugh and relax.

"Come, come, you must meet the cave people and get a drink!" Chelsea cried, opening the door to the outside. She worked at the ski resort and referred to her coworkers as "cave people" because their office was called "the cave."

Then, Chelsea began wrestling with some guy, and Linnea got a drink, still wondering why she had come to this party. She watched as her friend bounced around the deck, reaching up between each person's legs, flapping her arm like a fish, and yelling "salmon" for no clear reason at all.

Oh yes, Linnea thought. *Chelsea is why I came.* Her smile widened.

The cave people referred to Chelsea as the Poo Princess. Linnea laughed as her "salmon" turn arrived and then bear-hugged her. Then, the guy she had been wrestling with approached them and spoke to Linnea.

"What up? I'm Lan" He said, smiling.

"I'm Linnea."

"What do you do in town?" He asked.

She was about to respond when he suddenly interjected. "Wait! Holy shit! I know you!"

"You do?" And then she also remembered.

"We didn't exactly meet but we were on the lift together a few weeks back and we ..." They suddenly spoke in unison, "said a prayer for snow!"

For a second, the sky seemed to part as their eyes locked. But then, Lan stepped backward and his friend behind him bent over. Another dude pushed him and he fell back into the snow. He rolled out of it, got up laughing, and then threw snow all over his friends, moshing into them mischievously.

Unexpected attraction swept through Linnea. She looked again at the scruffy brown hair flooding out from his beanie. He wore overalls and looked goofy. His beard was scraggly and sparse like he had never shaved. He seemed too young, a kid almost; wresting with his friend like a man-child.

Linnea felt awkward, so she went to walk inside and pee. But Lan had noticed her leaving and came running after her.

"Wait! He called. "Linnea, right?" She was impressed he remembered her name already. Most people in town take forever to remember each others' names.

"I was just wondering..." He stopped awkwardly. "Do you, um, think our prayer actually worked?"

Linnea glanced around. Snow was falling like plumage after a pillow fight, and Lan's hat was speckled with sparkling down feathers. She smiled and put her hands up, catching some in the palm of her hand, as if to signify: well, *duh.*

"Well I think it did, but you tell me Mr, uh, Lan? What kind of name is that, anyway?"

"It's actually Ian. But my boss just thought the uppercase "I" was a lowercase "l" and ... you know how it goes, now my name is Lan." He shrugged and chuckled. "It's been so long that I have kind of just come to accept it. My boss gives everyone nicknames."

She laughed, "Ok ... Lan."

"Yes!" He then exclaimed, randomly.

"Yes, what?"

"I think the prayer worked." He almost looked guilty.

She then studied this elusive stranger with suspicion. Fate had somehow brought them together multiple times, and he was now foolishly smiling at her in the heavily falling snow. And then she felt a little panicked.

"I'm glad we met Lan, but if you'll excuse me, I have to use the restroom."

"Oh, yes, of course. I'm glad we met too." He then went back to his friends. She couldn't help but smile as she walked away.

After the bathroom, the night continued and Linnea ended up on the dance floor. The music was good enough that she could loosen, even surrender to the vibrations of sound. She and her girlfriends spun for fun and she found bliss. She loved dancing on the slopes and off.

The cave people, as they were called, all ended up inside too, wildly disrupting the dance floor. The guy who she had just met, who Chelsea kept calling "Lanyard," seemed to be really drunk suddenly. Linnea asked her about it and she said that Lan told her earlier he didn't eat dinner.

Ugh. *Men are so dumb*, Linnea thought. *So is drinking.* She decided she should probably be on her way then. She said bye to Chelsea and ghosted everyone else. She watched the snow fall in streetlights as she walked home; slightly buzzed, swearing off men and alcohol. He was cute though, or at least a lot cuter than Jack.

The lights outside the restaurant flickered through the swirling blizzard as they hurried inside. Lan, Pierce, and Couch Guy shook themselves like dogs in the lobby. They were starving.

"I don't want to talk about it," Pierce said to Lan.

"It's not like you even had to do anything," Lan laughed.

"I saw it, and that was enough to make me gag. I will have nightmares for a week."

"I was just trying to tell the Couch Guy about it." Lan protested.

"Enough! It's the last thing I want to talk about when we are about to eat!"

Lan had brought up "the tube of a thousand pubes," the plumbing coming out of the waterless urinal at the top of the tram. It clogs once a decade, and Lan had the pleasure of clearing it out with bowl patrol. Pierce stood in the background on the verge of vomiting, and one of the bowl patrollers actually did vomit. There was no denying: it was quite haunting.

Lan gave up and they went to sit at the bar. He then realized he recognized the server walking by.

"Linnea?"

"She smiled. "Oh hey, Lan!"

"I didn't know you worked here," Lan said enthusiastically, smiling back.

"Yeah. It's alright, pretty good money, but always so busy. You guys need a table?"

"Headed to the bar, I think."

She winked. "Okay, I will swing by in a few."

Lan was thrilled with excitement as they sat down — Linnea being there made everything better. He had wanted to talk to her more at the party, but things got a little out of hand with all of the cave people also being there.

"How do you know her?" Couch Guy asked with a nudge.

"Oh, I don't really know her yet. Kind of random, but we actually said a prayer for snow together on the lift a couple weeks ago."

"Lame," Pierce said quickly. He then called to the bartender, who was also Pierce's buddy.

Couch Guy spoke with less judgment: "That is pretty random, but I must say, she is a total babe."

She really was. Lan had been too drunk to really notice just how attractive she was the other night. He looked again at her across the distance. He found everything about her gorgeous: her dark long braid hanging down her right side, her work t-shirt tied in a knot around her belly. How had he met this girl?

"You have to admit, Pierce," Lan cheesed and looked over, "the prayer for snow did seem to work."

Pierce scoffed. "You seriously think you had anything to do with it?"

"I mean...."

"Well, I think you're an idiot," Pierce continued. "If you are so powerful, why don't you pray that this eviction just goes away?"

"That's not a bad idea," Lan joked.

He was going to ask more about the eviction, but just then Lan's phone buzzed in his pocket. He pulled it out and started texting a reply.

Couch Guy snickered, watching Lan use the nine digits on the phone to text. "I can't believe you still have that flip phone, Lan man," he said.

Lan looked at him with a grin. "You live on my couch, bro."

Pierce chimed in. "I can't believe I'm saying this, but I agree with the Couch Guy on this one. What's the deal dude? Just give in already."

"I guess I just don't agree with the vision of the future that has been forced upon us."

"Oh come on," Pierce replied.

"Seriously! We're stuck in this narrative that technology will fix all of the problems that our society has gotten itself into. Doesn't matter what side you take in this political madhouse, they both have the same vision of technological progress."

"The Singularity is near, Lan line." Couch Guy said with a wry smile.

"Um, what?" Pierce asked.

"Man and machine will soon merge," Couch Guy said, spookily.

Lan motioned towards the restaurant. "Who's to say they haven't already?" The three of them glanced around the restaurant. Almost every single person there was staring at their smartphone.

"It *is* kind of crazy." Couch Guy said slowly.

"It's like we are stuck in this Jetsons-based science fiction story about what the future will be and there is no alternative," Lan said with all seriousness.

"I think you're living in the past, Lan. You want to go back to the stone age." Pierce said.

"I didn't say that, but I do think there is plenty of wisdom to be gained from the past. Not everything has to be new, new, new. It's like technology has become our modern God."

"Well, Luddite Lan," Pierce said with a chuckle. "Why don't you go pray to a god you don't believe in that the science god will get destroyed?"

Lan glared at him, slightly offended. "I mean, maybe, obviously not to that God, but possibly to the old gods ... Hail to the old gods!" He poured a little beer out on the ground.

At that moment Linnea walked up to them, looking amused despite pretending to be disappointed.

"Hey!" She said with a smile. "Put that anywhere."

"Oh, sorry!" Lan got up quickly and wiped up the beer, clearly embarrassed. He continued. "Just hailing the old gods, y'know?" He winked. "You get out skiing today?"

She laughed at the comment. "Oh man, so epic! Sorry, I would have come over sooner, but it's just so busy tonight."

"Yeah, this place is packed." Lan looked around, feeling awkward.

"You guys hear the news?" she asked.

"Um, don't think so?"

"We are closing sometime in the next six months."

"What? Why?" they all asked.

"They are tearing it down," she said sadly.

Pierce spoke loudly, "No way! What are they putting in instead?"

"Luxury condos is what I heard, but that's just a rumor."

Pierce was really upset. "This fucking town, man. I'm telling you, the billionaires are doing their best to remove any semblance of culture."

"Who is living in the past now, Pierce?" Lan said with a cackle.

"Shove it, Lan."

"I'm joking! But seriously, welcome to the future."

Linnea smiled and Lan freaked out again. She spoke hurriedly. "You guys are funny! But, I'm sorry — I have to get back to a table."

She turned and walked away. Both Pierce and Couch Guy looked at Lan with wide eyes. Lan understood what they meant.

When Linnea looked less busy, he went over to her and asked if she wanted to ski sometime. She said yes, gave him her number, and told him she liked his phone. She was being serious, too.

"Nice work, bud," Pierce said, patting him on the back.

Lan was beyond ecstatic, but he had one more thing to say. "You know who is pushing this narrative of a sci-fi future more than anyone, Pierce?"

Pierce shrugged.

"The billionaires."

The skids went back to drinking, feeling a bit like victims.

Giggling, Linnea soared through the snow, letting her body move to the tempo of the forest. Her roommate, Sylvia, was a really good skier and was fun to go out with. Plus, they had been talking about mystical stuff all morning. Sylvia was into quantum physics, energy healing, psychedelics, and astrology. Linnea was really grateful to have her as a roommate.

Besides finding out that the restaurant she worked at was getting shut down, Linnea felt really intrigued by the magic of the world right now. She had something to be passionate about and felt less down on herself than last week. She hadn't drunk since the party, and she was also surprisingly electrified by this guy she kept running into.

It was odd — no, he was odd, or unique in a way. He still had an old flip phone, which was so weird. Linnea didn't even know people still possessed such things: even her parents had switched.

It all felt so coincidental, like the prayer they said on the lift somehow kept bringing them together. Her good friend, Chelsea, even worked with him. This was all besides the fact that she was actually attracted to him, even though, in some sense, he was still just another bro. And now, here he was, tall and handsome in his work uniform. He had texted earlier, and she'd agreed to meet up with him and Chelsea for a ski run.

"Hey Lan!" Linnea didn't mean to sound so excited. But he was smiling, and they hugged each other with the awkward hug of people holding skis and snowboards, their helmets banging together.

On the gondola, Lan told stories about work, including his adventures with an overflowing grease trap. None of his work stories sounded fun to Linnea at all.

"That's disgusting, dude," Sylvia said.

Chelsea then chimed in with a mischievous smile. "It wasn't so bad. We've dealt with worse." Her co-workers called her the Poo Princess specifically because she wasn't scared to get dirty.

Lan laughed. "Well, it's all about your attitude, right? When we're not shoveling gross stuff, we're shoveling snow. It's a great workout. Or we are fixing other stuff, so we learn a lot. And, I mean," and then Lan motioned with his arms, "look around." We are working right now, in the mountains, about to go ski powder, and I'm with all these beautiful ladies. Life's not so bad." Lan looked at Linnea when he said all this and then winked.

She felt herself blushing intensely, but luckily they were getting off the gondola. She and Sylvia followed Lan and Chelsea around for a run. Linnea did her best to keep up with Lan, and then suddenly realized she didn't want to follow him off a giant cliff. So, she turned abruptly and found a smaller one, laughing all the way.

He is crazy, she thought.

When they had finished, there were more awkward ski hugs, because Lan and Chelsea had to go to work.

Lan stumbled over his words briefly. "Anyway, I, um, uh, you're super cool, so I was thinking we should uh — talk? Like, have a real conversation sometime."

"Yes!" she smiled, blushing.

Lan smiled, too. "So, are you free tonight?"

Her face said no. "Oh, uh — unfortunately, I have to work the next couple of nights. But how about Monday?"

He looked enthused. "Okay, yes, yeah! So we will get to talk, like a real-life conversation, like real-life friends kind of thing, not just like 'oh hey yo what's up?'"

Linnea found his awkwardness funny! "Yeah — like real-life friends. I'd like that."

When Linnea told Sylvia later, Sylvia asked excitedly, "Are you saying he just asked you on a date?"

"Well," Linnea thought for a moment. "I mean, I guess? He said he wants to have a real-life conversation. We'll see." She was blushing again. Then, changing the topic, she said, "Anyway, I have to head down probably, get home, and go to work."

"Yeah," Sylvia said, laughing. "Just a conversation, huh? Well, I really wanted to show you something today. Have you seen the big crystal at the base of the mountain?"

Linnea hadn't, but then three thousand feet of blissful skiing later, she was staring at it with Sylvia. It seemed impossible she hadn't seen it yet nor had she even heard about it. Sticking out from the mountain, just a couple hundred yards above the base of the tram, was a massive quartz, jagged and shimmering.

The sun had just peaked out from behind the clouds as they skied up to it, and Linnea felt euphoric.

"It's kind of an anomaly," Sylvia said. "They think there was some sort of sinkhole, even the geologists can't explain it. This thing just came out of the ground. Talk about quantum energy. Something weird is going on."

Sylvia took her glove off and touched the glass-like face jutting into a point as tall as she was. Linnea touched it, too, and immediately saw what looked like swirled prisms of light beneath the surface, an array of colors that moved as she did. Little beads of dew covered it, while half-melted snowflakes revealed their own crystalline structure. The rock seemed to have been cut naturally into jagged corners. It looked like ice, as if carved from a glacier, but it was stone. A miniature mountain.

And, suddenly, Linnea thought she felt it vibrating. "Whoa," she said, and pulled her hand away. But then she wanted to feel it again, and so put her hand back to it.

Sylvia smiled. "You feel that, huh? I saw it a few days ago, and I really think it's a sign that some sort of bizarre energy is in the air. Did you know that the full moon falls on the winter solstice this year?"

Linnea kept her hand on the stone. There was definitely something inexplicable about it. It calmed her. She had a few crystals herself — her favorite was a stone from the top of the Grand Teton. But this was something else.

"I did!" she then said.

"I was thinking we could go to the hot springs and do a little ritual to embrace whatever celestial energy is influencing our terrestrial lives. You interested?" Sylvia asked.

"Count me in!" Linnea said, and then suddenly realized what day that would be. It was Monday, and that was her date with Lan. *Oh well*, she thought. *He can wait.* She needed her ladies' time. Especially on the solstice. Anyway, they literally had just hung out. But if she was really honest, she might have admitted she was also nervous. In fact, she thought maybe she might like him.

The snow just kept falling, and the coverage was incredible; a rare thing for this time of year. Some ski resorts have terrain parks, but this whole mountain was a terrain park. As Lan slid off a rock he was in awe of how much powder blanketed every surface. Even with the crowds, there was almost too much snow to get tracked out.

Linnea had rescheduled for another night, which was okay: she at least still wanted to meet up. She seemed genuine, so Lan tried to avoid overthinking it by skiing, his solution to most problems.

Lan wished he was working because he'd have more access to the slopes. The benefit of working for a ski resort was in the absence of rules that applied to you, at least in certain departments. People in black jackets could cut in front of every line, poach the soft closures (meaning no ropes), and hard closures (with intelligence), skiing all the untouched snow the tourists skied right past.

Lan had seen a few friends while skiing earlier that morning, but he had now lost them in the powder day frenzy. Nuking fat flakes created blind vertigo, every turn sending up a wave to impede vision. He wanted to find them again and get high, but he was near one of his favorite smoke shacks. So, instead, he dipped past a closed sign and headed for it.

Lan slid in and noticed some glass bottles in the corner next to a huge fur blanket. He hadn't seen those the other day — maybe someone else had come by recently. He started rolling but had to work fast because his fingers were already cold.

Suddenly, a strange feeling rushed through him. He strained his ears and thought he heard someone skiing up to the shack. "Fuck" he muttered to himself. Ski patrol wouldn't be so cool to him if he wasn't in uniform — this area was still closed.

Lan glanced through the window of the shack and saw what he thought was a kaleidoscope of colors in the snow. Then, he saw a big grey beard just before a huge man burst through the entrance. Furs and leathers and snow blasted into the doorway and Lan jumped back, cursing to himself. A booming laugh filled the small shack, and Lan shuddered.

Seconds felt like minutes as the two stared at each other. Every piece of the man's clothing was lined with fur and looked almost hand-made. Long fluffy ear flaps couldn't conceal his even longer hair — gold but streaked with grey — or his beard hanging down to his broad chest. The man had eyes like glacier ice, and Lan couldn't shake the impression that he was looking at a Viking on skis.

Lan stepped towards his board instinctively, preparing to leave, mildly afraid. But then the man said in a booming voice, "Happy solstice, young man."

Lan looked at him and said nothing except a barely audible "Huh?"

"You know ... winter solstice? The beginning of Yule? The longest night of the year?"

Lan barely understood the man's accent but picked up the meaning. "Oh — yeah, man, that's cool. I love the solstice, better thing to celebrate than Christmas."

"Drink?" The man pulled a glass bottle out of his coat pocket, matching the ones in the corner.

Lan held up the joint he'd been trying to roll. "Sure. Uh, spliff?"

The man nodded, then passed the bottle to Lan. Lan looked at the intricate tree etching on the bottle and then took a swig. It tasted like cold fire and burned as it went down.

"What is this stuff?" Lan asked, wincing.

"Aquavit ... the water of life. It's my own blend, I guess. Have more." The man took a long drag, and then another, then smoked most of it.

"Ah, okay." Lan didn't know what he had called the liquor; he looked with deep confusion at both the bottle and the tiny stub of the joint the man handed back. Then, he pulled out his phone to check the time. He flipped it open and then blinked hard against a blinding white light. It was broken.

"What is that?" the strange man said with amazement.

"Yeah, I dunno, I guess it's my phone. Seems a little fucked up right now. But that's okay. I don't want to have a phone. I feel like I'm in a techno dystopia where everyone is just staring at their phones all the fucking time. You know?" And then, noticing he was ranting, Lan asked, "You got a phone?"

The man smiled gruffly. "I do not have a phone."

Lan interjected excitedly, "Really? That's awesome!"

"... But I like yours," the man continued. "A techno dystopia — you are correct on that one, but you forgot the gnostic part." Then, suddenly, he added: "I need to go do one more lap before dark, because the solstice events must be prepared for."

"Oh!" Lan was feeling giddy, the accent was getting easier to understand. "Wanna shred with me?"

The man seemed confused, then suddenly replied, "Indeed, shred. We shall shred together."

Lan laughed and then looked at the man's massive wooden skis. "Those skis are huge! And wood? Bro, that is so sick! You're so — retro."

The older man replied, "Retro — yes, retro is good. The ski is an ancient technology full of myth and legend, a Stone Age tool. I like to appreciate it as such. I hope you can, too."

"A Stone Age tool — yeah, I never thought of it like that. I like it. Where did you even come from?" Lan said, feeling like the drink was kicking in strongly.

The man seemed briefly lost in thought before speaking. Lan thought he looked almost sad. Then, in his strange accent, the man finally said, "I ... I have been displaced from my homeland for now, like so many in this world."

"Displaced from home?" Lan said. "Oh shit! I am being evicted myself!"

"I feel we will all be back in our rightful place here soon," the peculiar man said eerily. "But for now, it is time to ride." He glanced at

Lan one last time, winked with those deep blue eyes which made Lan feel somehow colder, and said: "Swift, Silent, Deep."

Did he just reference the ski legends of Teton Hole? Lan was amazed — he'd just said their mantra. Stoke pulsed through Lan's veins in disbelief. He strapped in and followed his new friend into the forest.

Thinking he would have no trouble keeping up with this old man with wooden skis, he was baffled to find that was not the case. He rode as fast as he could and pushed himself to his limits.

A few thousand feet of powder riding later, the two looked like sliding snowmen. The man's beard was so plastered he could have been eating cake with no hands. Lan took his board off and laughed as he watched the snow fall from the man's long locks in heaves. The strange man then pulled skins from his fur coat and started putting them on his old skis.

"You're going back up? On skins?" Lan asked with surprise.

"I am indeed. It's the solstice, I must go light the Yule fires. Nice riding with you. We shall meet again soon. Keep up the trickery, I appreciate your lack of a smartphone, we will meet again soon. Strange times coming. Oh, and good luck tonight!"

"Tonight?" Lan wondered what he meant.

The massive man then began skinning back towards the hill. Lan gawked at him in disbelief. He suddenly decided he needed a photo of this guy, but it was getting dark.

He put down his backpack and pulled out his camera, then shouted "Yo, bro!" to get the man's attention.

The bearded man looked back briefly. Lan zoomed in and took his photo. The large, strange man then disappeared into the woods, leaving Lan standing there feeling like he was tripping. *What was in that damn drink?* Lan suddenly suspected it wasn't just booze.

The frosty air sparkled like glitter in the morning sunshine. Linnea walked outside her apartment and took a deep breath, adding her own frozen cloud to the atmosphere as she exhaled. Bailey bounded through the fresh snow with joy and left some of it marked with a yellow tinge.

Linnea reached over and picked up a handful of the cold confetti from the railing and then brought it up to her mouth. It melted onto her tongue, and she smiled. Solstice was one of her favorite days of the year.

She called her mom and wished her a happy solstice, her version of the holiday which had so clearly been co-opted. Her mom told her all about the festivities she would be missing out on, her brother was home and it would be great if she could make it sometime; but of course, it's so hard to get this time of year off of work. Maybe next year. She would probably have a different job.

What to do with such a beautiful day? She kind of wanted to keep reading her book about Norse mythology, but that could wait until after Solstice.

Sylvia was working and Chelsea was skiing. They all had plans to go to the hot springs later, but it was Linnea's first full day off in a while. Skiing recently was incredible, and she certainly had been taking advantage of it, but with the tourists showing up for Christmas she didn't want to deal with all that noise. Especially since it was the solstice, she wanted to be out in nature, in the woods in particular, with her dog, to enjoy some peace and quiet. Downhill skiing is great, of course, but it is so fast-paced sometimes: she wanted to move slowly today.

After breakfast, she gathered up all of her gear and drove to the pass. It was still snowing lightly, but the roads weren't too bad. Bailey was overly excited, jumping around the back seat. Linnea had put her skins on her skis at home so she slid into her boots and clicked in. She let Bailey out, put her on a leash until they got out of the parking lot, and then let her run free.

Linnea already felt better. Her skis zipped across the snow on the ground as more fell all around her. Bailey came bounding over, her black coat now white: she had found the deep stuff.

At that moment, a few skiers came flying down the cross-country track. She didn't need to deal with that right now; it was time to go off trail. Sure, it was deep, but one of Linnea's favorite things to do is to wander through the forest, at a nice slow pace, without any trail at all. Skis help with that in the winter.

So much of outdoor recreation requires you to have a goal, and a trail implies you are going somewhere. She thought that the only goal should be to wander aimlessly, taking in the beauty of her surroundings, with no rush. It seemed to her the best way to connect with the local spirits, the faeries of the wood.

The sound of trees creaking in deep cold surrounded her while snow fell like marshmallows. She took her time, Bailey's happiness enhanced her own, and the snow just kept falling.

After a while, she reached a clearing and decided this would be a good spot for a small ritual. Since it was the solstice, she wanted to do something to offer her gratitude to the land. She then burned some incense and poured some milk and honey out under a tree. She kept it simple and spoke aloud how appreciative she was of all the snow.

Suddenly, the mood shifted as a gust of wind swept through the clearing. The hair on her arms raised as she saw something out of the corner of her eye. Bailey growled. Linnea panicked and worried it was a moose.

Her heart beat quickly, thick fluff fell, the wind was now howling, and Linnea could see bright yellow eyes through the trees piercing her core as she reached down to get Bailey on her leash. A huge black wolf, just like the image from her dream, gazed back at her. Time became a long swirl of snow spirals, spinning Linnea's vision ever toward the center of those wolfish eyeballs.

She was terrified.

A skier then materialized out of the blizzard, directly behind the wolf. Linnea squinted through the storm and couldn't believe her eyes. The largest woman she had ever seen was on skis calling the wolf to her side. The wolf, which looked big before, now seemed smaller, like just a large black dog.

Bailey whined, and Linnea's blood slowed. She shivered and looked at the massive woman whose coat shimmered with something like sequins. Her long white hair was decorated with feathers and crystals, her entire body reverberated a glass-like aura mirroring spectrums of light back into the dark forest.

As Linnea made eye contact, the woman's cold eyes brought her warmth. Her smile seemed somehow to reflect off the snow all around them, and one side of her face was marked with tattoos.

"My dream," Linnea muttered. "I saw your wolf — or dog — in my dream."

The woman smiled again. "Dreams sometimes show the truth of what is to come." She spoke with a thick accent, almost German, yet it flowed like honey to Linnea's ears.

"Are you an angel?" Linnea questioned. "You are so beautiful!"

The woman kept smiling and sighed lightly. She seemed to ponder for a moment as if Linnea had asked her a difficult question.

"An angel?" The woman then glanced up at the sky. Large rugged snow slivers descended upon the two women with their canines by their sides. Linnea looked up as well. She felt ecstatic — she had never seen snow fall so hard. She focused, and her line of vision found a particularly exquisite snow crystal. When Linnea's eyes arrived on this flake, a memory abruptly flashed through her consciousness.

She remembered being a tiny, minuscule drop of water vapor, flying through the sky, growing from a single droplet into a flowering crystal of hexagonal snow falling through the air; swirling, floating, interlocking, and branching intricately.

After a wondrous moment, Linnea was back in her own body, watching the fernlike stellar dendrite of fantastic frost find its way to the forest floor already blanketed with its family.

The woman finally responded. "I'm not an angel, my dear, just a woman with somewhere to be. Happy Solstice."

Linnea stared in awe, unsure what had just happened in her mind. She looked at the dog again, and back at the sparkling woman. "Um, happy Solstice!" She said. "I don't want to keep you."

"You aren't. I am glad we ran into each other. I have a feeling I will see you again soon. In fact, I know it. The Solstice is a time of endings and beginnings."

This lady gets it. Linnea thought. But then the woman said something else, her light mood darkening as she spoke a different language. Linnea looked at her for a moment.

"I'm sorry what was that?"

"Fimbulwinter is coming," she said cryptically and then turned to ski away.

Linnea gasped in disbelief as the woman slid away on her skis. The dog turned and gave one last terrifying glance at Bailey. It was huge again, and not a dog at all but a massive wolf, and then it ran off to follow the mysterious woman disappearing into the forest.

Fimbulwinter? Wasn't I just reading about this?

Linnea stood there for a few seconds and then noticed something reflective in the snow where the woman had been standing. She skied over and saw the most incredible crystal. It was bright blue and had a shimmer to it like nothing Linnea had ever seen.

"Wait! You left this!" She cried out. But the woman was gone, her massive ski tracks already covered by the blizzard all around her. Linnea stood awkwardly in the quiet forest, holding what felt like a lost treasure.

Lan stared, confused, at the bright white screen on his camera. He had adjusted the exposure so that he could snap a shot of that man in the fading light. So, he had expected the photo to be slightly darker, not bright white. It was way over-exposed. Lan checked the settings again. The photo should have been fine, blurry maybe, but not like this.

The more Lan stared at the screen, the more he felt anxious. He remembered that his phone hadn't worked properly in the shack. It was functioning now but felt somehow wrong. He then realized that maybe his hands were what felt so peculiar. He held one up to his face as if he had never seen it before.

After a long moment of contemplation, Lan put the camera away and decided to go to the Cave to change. He kicked the snow gently as he walked through it, holding his board as he stumbled a little. Detailed patterns seemed to ride on everything he saw. Lan had walked this walk a million times, yet this time everything glimmered fantastically — so much more colorful than usual. People skied past Lan and it felt like they were flying up to him.

Oh man, he said to himself. *I'm fucked up.* A raven cawed above him, and he stared at it in amazement as it took flight. Dark wings reflected purple rainbows when it took off soaring towards the next building like it was some great castle. Ravens seemed to be everywhere, their screeches echoed dramatically. Lan shivered.

The door to the Cave looked like the entrance to a demented dungeon glowing under the orange light. He opened it and stepped through, calling out. He had expected to be bombarded with Cave people, but no one was there. The Cave was hardly devoid of life though — the ski signs littering the walls burst into three dimensional colors, moving in every direction. Lan stared in amazement, breathing slowly, watching the signs drift apart, and then back together like liquid puzzle pieces.

After some time studying the walls, Lan heard the door burst open from behind him, and five people came bounding in.

"Highlander! Lan-lock! Lanpoon! How's the day?"

Lan smiled and returned high fives. He then ran over to grab the ladder. He needed to change fast and get the hell out of there. Everyone coming in seemed to set him into panic mode.

"Oh, you know, nonstop Pow, man. May have hit the granny chutes...."

"What? You poached it? Sick!"

Lan thought about the strange dude he had met and wanted to tell them about him. But, considering how he was feeling — which was *crazy* — he decided he should wait. He changed out of his boots as fast as he could and told the Cave People, against their protest, that he had to be on his way.

Lan left the Cave feeling a little short. He had wanted to say more, but so many things were happening within his body that he was quite confused. He wondered if he might be tripping — he thought he could feel *all* of the energy around him.

Lan only felt like this on mushrooms. Then, he remembered the drink the Norwegian guy had given him with the tree engraved in the bottle and thought, *did that guy dose me?*

The wind was now blowing aggressively and snow flew from every direction. It was pure chaos and, besides the Christmas lights decorating the trees, it was entirely dark.

Lan felt better than he had in the Cave. Being in nature was much better for tripping than being indoors, and he watched the windy scene unfold in front of him with wonder. The roads looked blocked up with traffic, and he certainly didn't want to be on a bus right now.

He decided instead to go for a hike. Lan wandered up the hill and glanced into the forest. Oddly, as he looked through the trees, he thought he could see one of them glowing but not with Christmas lights. The more he looked at it, the more it looked like the tree from the bottle he had drank from: a massive evergreen.

He post-holed through the snow, struggling through the forest, wishing he had his split board. He was determined to get to that glowing tree. As he arrived at the base of it, out of breath, he fell down in awe.

He touched the Douglas fir slowly and then looked up. The tree had a slight bend in it as it climbed towards the heavens, but it wasn't glowing anymore. He closed his eyes, and then, even with them still closed, he thought he could still see it. Actually, he could see more, even its roots deep in the earth. As if hit by a cosmic train, he suddenly felt more connected to the universe than he ever had, like he was literally a part of this tree.

He opened his eyes and looked again. Lan could have sworn that it had been glowing when he had skied toward it, but now he understood he'd seen the full moon's light illuminating it from above. Just then, the moon seemed to shine brighter, and waves of feeling washed over him as the snowy branches danced in that light.

Lan sat by the tree and stared at it without any sense of the passing of time. He tried to think about all the problems of his life, but as chaotic as it all felt, the nonsense somehow flowed together seamlessly. In his current state, he couldn't help but embrace the mystery of it all.

There are so many possibilities, he thought. *They all branch out like … like a tree.*

He was excited to hang out with Linnea. He needed to figure this eviction thing out. He would find a new place to live. He wanted to keep living here because he wanted to hang out with Linnea. He wanted to stay.

The tree felt like a metaphor: grow but be rooted in place.

Lan felt the tree had become his new friend like it had been talking to him the entire time. And then he thought about the strange man. He still couldn't figure out why that photo of that dude didn't work, or what was in that drink. But it didn't matter: something had brought him clarity.

She gripped the steering wheel, driving through the blizzard with white knuckles. The flakes twinkled in the headlights like stars, trailing into the windshield as if, like in movies, they'd entered light-speed.

They were headed to the hot springs. The storm had picked up since Linnea left the pass — so much for being out under the full moon — and memories of her encounter with the woman and the wolf danced through Linnea's mind while she tried to stay focused on the road.

The three women smelled the sulfur from the springs as they descended the path. Between the steam and the snow, they could barely see the natural pools tucked into the side of the mighty snake river. Fortunately, it looked like no one was there and they could be alone in them.

Linnea, Chelsea, and Sylvia skipped lightly through the snow, and then they took their clothes off by the simmering ponds. With no one else there, they felt free to get naked. The steam rose as the storm raged, and flakes melted in mid-air above the pools. The three carefully climbed in after putting their dry clothes under their jackets. Naked as the snow was white, the hot water removed the last of their goosebumps, and they felt free.

"Happy solstice, everyone!" Linnea exclaimed.

The ladies all cheered as Chelsea passed a bag of wine around and filled the cups they'd brought. Linnea poured a small amount out into the water as an offering. Chelsea laughed at her, shaking her head slightly.

"What? The solstice is a holy time for many pagan peoples." She said.

"I wasn't complaining!" Chelsea put her hands up.

"It's the longest night of the year," Sylvia added with a smile.

"Exactly! The darkness reigns at this period, the sun has died." The girls laughed again. Linnea then added. "But seriously, did you know the Solstice is actually a bit of an apocalyptic event?"

"Certainly been feeling apocalyptic with all the nonsense in politics recently. Seems like the world is about to end," Sylvia joked.

Linnea laughed. "No doubt there, but did you also know that the word 'apocalypse' actually doesn't mean the end of the world? But instead means something hidden will be uncovered, unveiled, revealed."

"Like the sun?" Chelsea smiled.

"Exactly. The seasons of the year are a cyclical thing, not a linear thing. We are kind of stuck in a Christian story of apocalypse where the end of the world means the end of time, the earth will be destroyed and only the chosen few will get to go to heaven. But in a pagan worldview the darkness of winter brings the death of the sun, except before she dies, she gives birth to a new sun. The earth is cleansed of its corruption, and it's also reborn, not abandoned. The Norse peoples called this event the *Ragnarök.*"

"Oooh," Sylvia said with excitement. "I like the way that sounds. But tonight is a full moon, doesn't that mean this solstice is different, like, not so dark?"

"Maybe?" Linnea said, feeling hopeful. She looked up at the snow falling from the sky, peppering their hair before melting, the moon somewhere above the storm.

"Too bad we can't see it," Sylvia added.

"Too bad?" Chelsea said. "Fine by me. It's snowing so much! This storm has been apocalyptic. A snow-pocalypse!" she yelled.

Linnea felt like everything was suddenly falling into place and made perfect sense. She was literally just reading about this, and that woman had then somehow mentioned it.

Linnea continued, a half-formed memory stalking her thoughts. "I wonder if that's synchronicity. There is supposed to be a big storm that precedes the *Ragnarök.* A multiple-year storm where even the summers are snowy."

"Multiple years? Yeah right, not with how things have been lately. The Earth is too warm." Sylvia replied.

"I know..." Linnea said, her voice trailing off. She suddenly couldn't get an image out of her mind; the massive woman with a wolf standing next to her. She'd said something about "Fimbulwinter...."

"Wow," Sylvia exclaimed suddenly, pulling Linnea from her thoughts. "That thing is crazy!" She was staring at the crystal Linnea had found after that strange woman had left. "Where did you find that?"

"This woman I met, she dropped it. It kind of reminds me of the crystal at the ski resort, the one you said was a geological anomaly. They both have this subtle glow to them, almost supernatural."

The girls passed the crystal around in silence. Linnea then asked. "So, are we going to do our little ritual, or what?"

Chelsea sighed, a little hesitant, but agreed.

Sylvia said "Yes!" joyously and continued. "Obviously this storm is unreal, but I have a feeling if we do a little meditation, the moon may bless us with her presence, if only for a moment."

Sylvia passed around some lavender essential oil. "I brought some candles, too, but I don't think they'll stay lit in this snow. Authentic simplicity, right?" She smiled at Linnea and continued, "I just want to say thanks for being willing to do this little ritual tonight. I really need this in my life right now. I think it is really important for women to have spaces where we can just be ourselves sometimes."

They dabbed the oil on their skin while Sylvia gave them instructions. "Just relax and take deep breaths, close your eyes, and clear your mind," she said, and then she told them to join hands and visualize their chakras vibrating with earth and solar energy.

Linnea was having a hard time focusing, though. She tried to follow Sylvia's instructions, but her head was instead full of images of that wolf and the sparkling woman. All the while, the snow continued to pelt her face, which only distracted her even more.

Sylvia then suggested they all choose an intention to focus upon for the upcoming year, or maybe a dream they had, and to imagine it already being accomplished.

The silent sound of snow falling was accompanied by the trickle of the river, and Linnea clutched her new crystal in her hand under the water. She was imagining herself pursuing her magical practice this year, being like the snowflake she had experienced earlier, being like the mysterious woman from the forest.

Linnea suddenly remembered a dream she'd had. It was a terrible dream, a nightmare, and now she was back in it. She was on top of the tram in the middle of winter, smoke was everywhere, and there was no snow.

And then she remembered what the woman had said: "Dreams sometimes show the truth of what is to come."

No, Linnea thought to herself.

"We are light," Sylvia said, still leading them. "The light is returning, the sun being reborn...." But Linnea saw again the entire mountain and all the land around it on fire.

"No!" she shouted, startling the others. Linnea opened her eyes and was blinded. The moon was shining through the clouds, lighting up the landscape as if it were daytime.

"Are you okay?" Sylvia asked with concern.

Linnea exhaled and calmed herself. "Oh, I'm fine, sorry! A bad dream suddenly came back to me."

Sylvia looked worried. "A bad dream? About what?"

The snow had stopped falling and Linnea looked at her two best friends. "About there being no more snow," she started and then stopped. She'd heard a noise, the same one her friends had just heard, too.

"There goes our girls-only space," Chelsea groaned. They all looked up at once and sighed, watching a large group of dudes descending the trail towards them.

PART II:
ALTERED STATES

17: The Nightmare After Christmas

Sasha awoke in a sweat. His heart was pounding and his mind was filled with terrible visions. He jumped up in a fit of confusion and tried to remember where he was.

He looked around and let the familiar surroundings calm him. He was in his apartment, in San Francisco, with a view over the city. In his dream, on the other hand, he had been back in Teton Hole, outside one of his rental properties, the ugly brown one. He had been standing next to his father in its driveway, surrounded by wolves that howled and yelped while they circled around them.

But worst of all was that man. Demonic, terrible, with antlers coming out of his head, the man had walked out of the darkness directly towards Sasha and his dad.

"It is not yours," the devilish being had said. "Not anymore."

Sasha had protested but was ignored. The demonic man said something about giving it back to better caretakers of the land, but Sasha couldn't hear what else he said. While the demon talked, the howling of the wolves got louder, and louder like they were celebrating an impending kill. Terrified, Sasha had frozen and then fell to the ground in a fetal position, awaiting his fate.

And then he had jumped awake, still terrified. He tried to understand what he'd seen — it had felt so real like he was really there. But why was his father also there? Sasha wondered if it had something to do with his father's non-profit, the one committed to greening Teton Hole. Or maybe it was just because they were selling the house?

Sasha didn't want to feel guilty. His whole passion in life was finding technology that would help nature. And it was his dad's idea — no, his insistence — to sell the house, not his. But also, his dad was funding all his research, and helping him to find more funding, and he was right: the land that house was on was worth much more than he could ever get for it in rent. Still, he didn't feel like just kicking people out like that.

Sasha's phone rang. He fumbled for it, looked at the screen, and then dropped it.

The call was from one of his tenants in Teton Hole. It was from Pierce, the one who was on the lease at the Brown House he had just been dreaming about.

Sasha didn't answer. It was too weird. He let the call go to voicemail and then listened to the message.

"Hey man, um, yeah, man. This is Pierce from the, uh, Brown House. Can you just maybe call me back, man? We were really thrown off by the eviction thing and I still haven't heard back from you about it which is pretty weird, man. So, yeah, can you just call back? Please?"

Sasha couldn't believe the coincidence. The dream, the phone call, it was all too much. He wasn't as religious as his father was, but he couldn't help but feel like there was some sort of message coming through, a warning from God himself. At least he hoped it was from God, because that demon man in the dream terrified him.

Was Satan coming after him because he hadn't devoted himself to the church like his father kept telling him to? He had always considered himself an atheist: he believed in science and that the enlightenment had disproved God's existence. But this dream felt too real, his body would palpitate each time he recounted it.

Sasha had to meet his father in Teton Hole in six weeks. There was a meeting about the non-profit, but he suddenly felt like he needed to get there as soon as possible, like somehow it would help him resolve this conflict. He could easily work remotely, so he booked the next flight to Wydaho, and then he got down on his knees to pray.

The problem was that he wasn't exactly sure who he was praying to.

The streets had been carved into epic canyons meandering through mountainous snowbanks. Linnea and Lan stepped onto the neighborhood road and, walking side by side down the snowy trench, furtively glanced at each other.

Linnea thought she had probably blushed when they made eye contact, but luckily it was dark so Lan probably couldn't see it. The snow fell pleasantly as they strolled, and Linnea felt both nervous and electric, especially every time they "accidentally" brushed shoulders.

This date — that was "not a date" — was sure feeling like a date.

"Thanks for being down to walk," she said.

"Are you kidding?" Lan replied enthusiastically, "It's way too nice out to drive and parking downtown in winter is absurd."

"Thanks for making reservations, too. I'm honestly surprised you were able to get any on Christmas Eve."

"Yule Eve!" Lan said.

She smiled and responded. "You are so right!" *Did he actually say that just now? She was ecstatic.*

She had dressed up slightly but had tried not to overdo it. It wasn't supposed to be a date, it was supposed to be a way for them to have a real-life conversation and be real-life friends. Entering the restaurant, she took off her jacket and hung it on the coat rack. Lan did the same and then looked over at her sheepishly.

After an awkward moment of him looking at her like that, she said: "What?"

"Oh, nothing. Sorry. It's just your hair, is it always this curly?"

"No." She blushed. "I, um, I curled it."

"Well, I like it." He said this and something about his smile made her nerves skyrocket again.

They sat down at a table in the bar section. They had come to a locally-owned place ironically named "Local."

"Do you ever go out ski touring?" Lan asked her.

"I do!" She was relieved to be sitting down. "I need to go more, I took my avalanche safety course a few years ago, but I could always use more people to go with. It's a bit intimidating."

"I totally get it. Avalanches are scary. The spirit of the mountains can be intense. But if you pay attention to the snowpack, you can make safe decisions. I would love to take you out sometime. It is really nice to get out skiing without all the craziness of the resort. Now that the holidays are here, it's too busy. Have you ever toured in the Tetons?" he asked.

"Oh, I have done a little, but nothing too wild. It is so beautiful up there. Do you do that? You seem like a really good snowboarder."

"I mean, yeah, I do, but I haven't skied the grand or anything, just the middle...."

"Oh, wow, you're crazy." She'd been looking into his eyes and was starting to feel lost in them. Quickly, she averted them back down to the menu.

Lan broke her sudden awkward silence. "Anyway, how long have you been working at that restaurant? That is such a bummer it's shutting down."

"I know — I have been there a few years now, but I honestly would like to do something else. I kind of want to work for this non-profit in town that rescues all of the expired food from grocery stores and restaurants. They then redistribute it to the community, to the people who need it the most. I just want to do something of service to the community, not just serve the tourists, y'know?"

"Nice!" He replied. "I have heard of that and have wanted to get involved. So cool. Did you study something like that in school?"

"Not exactly, I was an environmental studies major," Linnea said, mildly trailing off because she never pursued it after school.

"No way!" Lan seemed really impressed. "I studied sociology, but environmental studies was a huge part of it. I found it almost too interesting. How does society treat the environment?"

Linnea laughed and sighed slightly. "Yeah, it's honestly kind of depressing; the answer is they don't treat it very well. I wanted to get a job in the field but recently I have been feeling a little...."

"Hopeless?" Lan suggested with a smile and a shrug.

"No — I mean, yeah, maybe."

"It seems like the narrative surrounding climate change has shifted here in the last few years. Clearly, the politics are all fucked." Lan said.

"Is that how you feel about it?" Linnea asked him suddenly. "Hopeless, I mean?"

"Oh. I don't know. I was so excited about being an activist for a while and I did participate, but that form of action seems to have little effect anymore. The funny thing is, everyone believes in science, right? We literally restructured our entire society during covid in the name of believing in science. But climate change science has been around for fifty-plus years and restructuring society based on that science is seen as crazy, labeled too idealist. The facts don't change how we live." Lan said a little sadly.

"That's a good point," Linnea added. "I guess I have just come to think about it in terms of, 'what can we do in our own lives?'"

"Oh, totally," Lan perked up, "I agree, but our individual impact is honestly pretty small, the biggest polluters are major corporations, who often set up their factories abroad to avoid regulations. Oh, and the military is actually the world's largest polluter, and very destructive to the environment, but these things are rarely talked about. They like to blame the common person to make us feel guilty. If only we could recycle more. Or vote harder."

Linnea laughed. *He is actually pretty smart,* she thought. "You are right about that. Unfortunately, we treat our resources as if they were limitless, it is this idea of an infinite economy which is the base problem...."

She was going to keep talking but Lan suddenly looked at her the way he had earlier when she had taken off her coat. It was as if she had said something he hadn't expected.

"What?" She said again with mild embarrassment.

He laughed out loud and responded, "Sorry, I just noticed you referenced the infinite growth economy as the base problem of climate change. Usually, I am the one bringing up capitalism."

She chuckled and looked back at him. Waves of emotion she could only understand to be good were moving through her. As the waves crashed, it was almost too much to take in.

She broke the silence this time. "It is true, though. I mean, the economy seems like something too big to change, but a girl can dream, right?"

"Damn right, you can! I, um, like to embody the trickster archetype. It's a forty-thousand-year-old myth. And usually, the gods rule the world right? But tricksters are always in the background, always mixing things up, steering things in new directions. Messing with the gods' plans. Making anything possible." Lan said.

"Ooh. I love that." She replied.

"I must say, you are pretty fucking cool," he suddenly stated.

"Oh, thanks." She put her hands in a flat line under her face, trying to be cute. He laughed.

"How did we meet again?" Lan asked a bit rhetorically. Before she could respond he continued. "I have been meaning to ask you. Do you, um, actually think...?" He was hesitating.

"Do I think what?"

"Do you think the prayer we said actually did something?"

She was suddenly brimming. "Well, of course! Do you not?"

He laughed. "I mean, yeah, no, I mean, yeah. I want to believe it did something, well, clearly because it has snowed absurd amounts since that day, but I guess I have a hard time with the vanity aspect, like, do you really think it is all because of us? All of this snow?" He waved his arms out as if the whole restaurant was full of it.

"Well, Lan," she liked where this was going. "I believe that we all manifest our realities to some extent, right? So putting our prayer out there may seem like a small act that really doesn't affect the big wide world. But according to quantum physics, we are in a constant energy exchange with the universe. Things aren't as separate as Newtonian physics has led us to believe. We kind of exist in this invisible web, right? A field. It is constantly in motion, it is a heaving sea of energy made up of microscopic vibrations. The craziest part is, particles are able to influence each other over vast distances. So our prayer is actually interconnected to the rest of the cosmic sea. The real question is: how could it not do something?"

"Um, boom," Lan said.

She laughed and added one more thing. "I don't think this storm is solely because of us, of course." The image of the woman in the forest flashed through her mind again. "But we certainly helped. I think ritual is key to taking action." She smiled, matter-of-factly.

When Linnea finished talking, she noticed Lan was once again staring at her with that strange look on his face. He was partially smiling, but looking directly into her eyes with an intensity she didn't quite know how to deal with. His blue eyes seemed to be brighter than anything else in the room with the way they contrasted his face. She thought she could sense energy moving extremely quickly between the two of them.

"Stop that!" She blushed and looked away. She looked back and he was beaming.

He replied, "Sorry! I just really liked what you were saying, that's all! No one ever talks to me about quantum physics!"

The conversation only got better as they ate and drank. They seemed to agree on a spiritual path forward for humanity, but also for the other-than-human, and human potential beyond merely advancing technology. And it all felt so casual to talk this way with him. Linnea was starting to let down her guard. She really liked the way he looked at her.

Lan walked her home in the lightly falling snow, snow they had both helped fall from the sky. When he reached for her hand, Linnea asked if "real-life friends" were supposed to hold hands. He said it was allowed. She felt more and more energy between them, especially when they looked at each other.

Outside her place, as the waning moon peaked through the cloudy sky, she kissed him and then said goodnight.

The sunset exploded fire across the sky as Lan was changing the trash at the end of the day. He was wet and tired and a little cold — but none of that really mattered. Life felt really good. He had ridden epic powder all day on Christmas, or Yule that is, and the night before had been the best night ever.

He looked towards the forest in the distance and remembered his experience from the other night, his strange and profound connection with that tree. Ever since then, everything seemed to be falling into place perfectly. Everything, of course, besides the eviction.

"So he hasn't called you back?" Lan said to Pierce as they sat down at the bar. The Moose was the only place open, and even that was surprising for Christmas day. Lan didn't need to be spending more money, but the three of them needed to talk.

"Nope."

"Well, what did you say?" asked the Couch Guy.

"I uh, well, I told him he had to call me back and that we were really thrown off by the eviction and yeah, to call me back."

Couch Guy jumped in. "Nah, man. You need to threaten him. What he did was fucked up. We can't just let him get away with this."

"Threaten him? *We?*" Pierce was upset. "Dude, you don't even pay rent! I'm the one on the lease."

Couch Guy replied. "That's why I feel like I gotta do something, like to make up for it, y'know?"

"Well, you could start by actually paying us for the last few months you have been sleeping on the couch," Pierce said, obviously frustrated. Lan laughed.

Couch Guy responded. "No, no, no. I have a better idea. Legally he is not.... "

Pierce then interrupted. "Dude. Whatever your idea is, don't do it. You will fuck it up worse than it already is. I might just end up leaving town anyway, guys. I am pretty much over this place, even with the snow. All the chicks just use me for sex and move on. They think of me as their fuck boy."

Lan laughed slightly, "What happened to Tracy?"

"Oh, she said she was getting back with her boyfriend. I don't want to talk about it." Pierce seemed bummed.

"It'll be ok, bud. Why don't you give me the landlord's number? I'll call him a million times if I have to. There is no way we will be moving out next fucking week for 'distributing peace.' That can't be legal."

Lan felt like he had to do something. Life may mostly be going extremely well recently, but he realized he had been far too passive in this situation.

Pierce responded angrily, "Fine. I'm sure you guys can all suddenly do a much better job than me. I have been trying to call him for weeks now. Sorry that I haven't threatened him...." He waved his hands in the air.

"Whatever, dude, I'm not trying to be a dick about it," Lan butted in again. "We are in the right here, not him. It's what they want. They want us divided and fighting amongst ourselves."

Pierce made a confused face. "Who is 'they,' Lan?"

"The landlords, all of them! This guy thinks he can just evict us in the middle of winter with some half-assed note and not even communicate with us in any other way? I mean, this whole town's living situation is not ok. These billionaires have fucked us. Leaving town won't do shit about it. We need to stick together."

"Wow. Now I'm all hot and bothered and inspired and need a shot because you guys are my favorite idiots around." Pierce laughed. "Well, at least you are my favorite idiot, Lan. This damn Couch Guy can suck it." Pierce then waved toward the bartender and asked for a round of shots.

"What kind?"

"Ullr?" Pierce looked around for agreement, seeming calmer already.

Lan watched as the bartender poured the shots with interest. "Wait, can I look at that bottle real fast?" Lan held the bottle in his hand with a strange euphoric feeling. It was a peppermint schnapps, and it had a little symbol of a guy on skis holding a bow and arrow. The bottle also had a little poem about Ullr on the front and a prayer for snow on the back.

"What's up, little Lantern? You've never had Ullr before?"

"No, I have. It just reminds me of...." Lan didn't see the point in explaining. "Whatever. Let's just take the shot. Fuck the landlords, right?" Lan held up his glass.

"Fuck the landlords!" they said in unison.

"Speaking of fucking...." Couch Guy said. "Lan, didn't you go on a date last night?"

"It wasn't exactly a date," Lan said. "And it wasn't like that. But it was awesome."

"So you didn't hook up?" Pierce asked.

"No — but this girl, she just — gets it, y'know?"

"Gets what?" Pierce asked.

"The deeper level, dude. Like how we are treating the Earth, how we can live differently, not be so sucked into the propaganda. I honestly haven't had a conversation like that in a long time, man. She is a dreamer."

"Fuck yeah, bud!" Couch Guy exclaimed.

"Lame," Pierce shrugged.

Lan already felt a strong buzz from the drink, and it reminded him of the liquor the Viking man in the shack had given him, though it was much different. He still wasn't sure whether or not there'd been something else in that drink, but he really craved that feeling again.

Linnea lit a candle in the dark of morning, set out her cushion, and sat down to do a little meditation. She pulled a Tarot card, placed the blue quartz crystal next to the candle, and focused on it as she breathed. She closed her eyes and performed the rainbow chakra meditation Sylvia had taught them at the hot springs. Everything in her relaxed as she breathed in and out. Light flowed through her and cleansed her body, and she felt connected to the cosmos. She searched for the void. Ritual was what she needed. Ritual was her new pursuit.

In this calm and meditative state, she suddenly remembered the dream she had the night before. It was weird — what had she been doing? Ice skating?

"Ok, well, before we ski," Linnea later said to Sylvia after walking Bailey. "I had this dream — oh, never mind. I was thinking we should go ice skating! There is a rink out at the village, right?"

"Ok ... I kind of suck, but I could be convinced!" Sylvia responded with a smile.

"If you can ski, you can skate, right?" Linnea said optimistically. Sylvia laughed and they headed towards the village. The traffic was terrible, but they had at least found good spots on the bus and could sit. All the tourists were in town, and the bus provided quite entertaining people-watching. Gapers were out in full, their goggles falling off the back of their helmets, dropping their skis on Sylvia, and being generally unaware of everything around them.

When the girls finally made it out to the resort, the ski lines were outrageous. Normally, this would have been frustrating, but luckily, they had dream-inspired plans. They rented ice skates and found their way onto the rink. It had snowed the night before, but the rink had already been shoveled off and the girls were some of the only ones on it.

Linnea felt ecstatic as she glided around the rink, her hair flapping out behind her as she went faster. Sylvia gave her a holler as she watched from her slower-moving location.

Linnea looped back around, crossing one leg over the other. Moving her body was always one of the best ways to feel better. For many people and other animals, winter is a time for hibernation, and as much as Linnea absolutely loved hibernating a good bit in winter, getting out and moving around in the snow seemed to make more sense to her. It had occurred to her that if you live in a place that is cold and has snow you should go out and play in it. If you don't go out and play in the snow, then you are just cold.

"Damn Linnea, you look good out there."

"Thanks..." she beamed. "I used to skate a lot in high school." She couldn't stop smiling.

"You seem so happy!" Sylvia exclaimed. "What has gotten into you?"

Linnea couldn't hold it in. "I just had so much fun on this..." she couldn't deny it any longer, "this date with this guy the other night, and ever since then...."

"Why didn't you tell me?" Sylvia smiled and clapped her hands.

"I haven't known what to think about it all, but I guess the one thing I do know is that I have been happy, I guess I kind of like this guy."

"Seems like more than 'kind of!" Sylvia joked.

Linnea continued to smile as she took off for another lap around the rink. She was embarrassed in the best way possible. She never felt this way! They skated a bit more until a huge gust of wind came hurtling through the rink. A swirling flurry enveloped them, and it looked like the storm had picked up. Five minutes later the snow was piling onto the rink; the girls could barely see.

They changed back into their ski boots and walked towards the tram in the howling blizzard. The women pulled their goggles down as snow pelted their faces with intensity. Linnea turned and looked back at the rink, and she suddenly noticed a woman skating there. She hadn't been on the rink when they were, but she looked familiar.

Pointing, Linnea yelled through the wind at Sylvia. "Do you see that woman?"

"What? Sorry, I can't hear you! I really have to pee!" Sylvia had put her skis down and was motioning that she was headed down the stairs to the bathroom. Linnea looked again and watched the woman skate like there wasn't even a blizzard at all.

Linnea recognized her — she was the woman from the other day. She ran up to her, and just as she did the storm seemed to calm around them, the snow falling more slowly.

Linnea called out. "Hey! It's you, the woman from the forest!"

The woman looked over and stopped her glide. She smiled and approached. Linnea was once again taken in by the woman's look. Her hair was ridiculously beautiful — white, with braids and feathers interspersed. Linnea had never seen someone do that with their hair, or definitely not so well!

"Hello, again" the woman spoke a sparkling smile in her German accent. "It is good to see you again, dear one."

"I have your crystal! I mean, not here, but at home."

"Oh, good. I had hoped you had found that."

"You lost it," Linnea said, a bit confused by the woman's response.

"I did, but I am glad you found it. You keep it for now. Let it be a reminder to you of all that is magical in this world."

"Okay." A creeping sensation flowed through Linnea. "Thank you." Then, fumbling for words, Linnea added, "Sorry, I just kind of bounded over to you, I just ... you seem really neat."

Linnea then noticed something out of the corner of her eye and jumped. Just beyond them in the woods, crouching in the thick trees, was the large black wolf. She had put her hand to her chest in shock, but when she looked back at the massive woman, she felt suddenly calm again.

"You're the wildest person I have ever met," Linnea said, almost entranced.

"I appreciate all of your kind words," the woman said and looked as if she meant to say more. But instead, she started coughing intensely like she was gasping for air.

"Are you okay?" Linnea asked.

Linnea waited, worried. The woman kept coughing and gasping, and then, after what seemed like several minutes, finally recovered.

The woman then nodded her head and said, "Yes, I am okay, thank you. I was about to say I appreciate your kind words, but my presence and wildness serve a purpose."

Linnea paused to think about this, then asked, "Can I ask you a question?"

The woman smiled lightly and nodded.

Linnea was nervous. "My girlfriend and I are starting to get into doing, um ... rituals. Sorry! I'm totally embarrassing myself here. But you seem — do you ever ... do you ever do any rituals, too?"

The massive woman laughed. "It is a good question. I am actually here to do a ritual on New Year's Day by the large stone at the base of the cliff. It will be the new moon. Would you like to join me?"

Linnea nodded but then heard Sylvia calling out for her. "One moment, sorry. Be right back — my friend is looking for me."

When Linnea had found Sylvia, she could barely form her sentences. "Guess what! I just ran into the most magical lady ever, she looks like a snow queen witch giant!"

Sylvia laughed but looked confused. "Okay? Where?"

Linnea turned and pointed back at the ice rink, but the woman had already left.

"Uh — she invited us, or me at least, to do a ritual with her on New Year's Day! Do you want to go?"

"Oh, Nea, that sounds incredible, but I am flying home that day, remember?"

Linnea searched a bit more for the strange woman, but to no avail. She and Sylvia then skied some, but Linnea couldn't get the woman out of her mind. She talked about her, and then also about Lan, and she found herself constantly smiling. Everything seemed too good to be true.

Besides one thing, that is. Linnea couldn't stop thinking about that lady's cough. It seemed like she was sick or something. And then Linnea realized she needed to remember to ask her name the next time they met.

The woman hadn't given her her phone number, either. In fact, all she had said was a time and a place.

Couch Guy did a few ski runs in the morning with Pierce, and then told him he needed to leave to "get some shit done." Pierce had then tried to point out how he didn't actually *ever* have anything important to do, but he persisted.

He was happy for any excuse to walk his dog, Roscoe. The large white Malamute bounded down the street with glee, happily sniffing anything that looked like old piss and contributing his own fresh scent to the yellow snow. After walking to the other side of town, and then up a long long hill, Couch Guy looked at his phone and back at the house in front of him, his real destination.

If this is where the Landlord lives, Couch Guy thought, staring at the mansion, *he must be loaded.* A cyber truck sat in the driveway. Couch Guy suddenly had a burst of confidence. *I can do this.*

His frayed snow pants dragged in the snow as he trudged his way up to the front door of the massive house, with Roscoe following alongside. He knocked and then suddenly realized how ridiculous and poor he probably looked.

The door opened slowly. A clean-shaven man, maybe in his late thirties, peered out suspiciously. He then seemed to relax like he was relieved it wasn't someone more important.

"Can I help you?" the man asked as he opened the door all the way.

Roscoe, who of course wasn't on a leash, must have seen something inside the house because he started barking and ran inside past the landlord.

"Roscoe!" Couch Guy yelled. "Get your ass back here right now!"

Roscoe heard but was not one to listen. Couch Guy called his name a few more times and decided to let himself in, brushing past the landlord. "Sorry man, I will get him right out."

"Uh ... my cat." The man clearly wasn't sure what to do.

Couch Guy walked into the large house, and could hear Roscoe running and slipping on the hardwood floor in the room next door. Roscoe was definitely chasing a cat, and he heard him run into a room across from the kitchen. Couch Guy followed him in, then saw the cat must have hidden under a couch.

Grabbing Roscoe's collar, he caught a glimpse of the rest of the room and then froze. On a table nearby, he saw a pile of small remote drones, some camera gear, and a bunch of other equipment he didn't understand. Near the table was a desk with several giant computer monitors. *Dude is really into tech,* Couch Guy thought.

The landlord entered behind him, and Couch Guy tried to act like he hadn't been staring at anything at all. The landlord looked quite upset. "And once again, hello. Why are you here?"

"Oh yeah, man. Sorry, dude. I just wanted to talk to you about your tenants over at the Brown House. I don't think what you're doing is all that cool, man. Eviction in winter? Pretty lame. It was just Christmas, bro." Couch Guy said in a slightly stoned voice.

The landlord shrugged. "Well, the house is already for sale, and I'm within my rights to do this. Do you live there as well? I don't recognize you — you're not on the lease."

"Me? Um, no ... Nope. I just, uh — I am their legal advisor."

The landlord chuckled slightly, obviously amused.

Couch Guy then pulled out the lease and the eviction notice he had taken from Pierce. "For one, these tenants are on the lease until the end of May. Why not wait until then instead of breaking the lease? It's winter, dude."

The landlord started to speak, but Couch Guy continued.

"Now we also have your so-called 'eviction notice,' which if you look closely, is clearly not a legal document. For one, you meant to put your reason for eviction being 'disturbing the peace.' But you have a typo here and it says that the tenants were merely 'distributing the peace,' which makes this all, uh, void. Also, state law says you need a Writ of Restitution or a Notice to Quit, and if the landlord is the one breaking the lease, at least thirty days is allowed for the tenants to vacate the premises, and you didn't give them either of these."

The landlord looked blankly at him, and Couch Guy wasn't sure what else to say.

"So," he added. "Do I need to call my lawyer or what?"

The landlord shook his head. "I thought you said *you* were their legal adviser?"

Couch Guy turned nervously back towards the still-open front door, and then smiled. Roscoe was now outside, shitting on the steps of the man's house. Couch Guy stepped outside and petted him on the head.

He then turned back towards the landlord and gave him a serious nod. "That's right. So do we have an agreement?"

The landlord said nothing and then closed the door.

Lan picked a piece of ice out of his mustache with his tongue. The rest of his face was covered in snow sticking to his goggles like plaster. Though he could barely see, he could hear the excitement of everyone around him, cheering, celebrating the immense fall of snow from the skies. This year, even with its weird start, had turned out to be epic. It was a fantasy powder wonderland.

Lan knew he was once again letting the snow distract him from taking action in life, but he wasn't about to let the anxiety overwhelm him. He could do it.

He called the landlord.

"Hey Sasha? This is Lan, your tenant in the Brown House."

"Oh hey, Lan. Funny you called. "Your friend, or legal advisor, or whoever was just here at my house."

Lan didn't know who he was talking about, so didn't reply.

"I just got off the phone with Pierce, as well. There was a typo on the notice, I apologize. But I've decided to give you more time to figure something else out."

Lan barely muttered a "thank you" before Sasha hung up. He then called Pierce.

"I'm going to kill him," Pierce said on the phone. "I told him not to get involved!"

"You can't be that upset, the Couch Guy got us more time!"

"I can be upset if I want to. Who does he think he is? The nerve to do such a thing! Fucking idiot."

"Just try and relax, bro. We're good for now, it's a pow day, where are you?"

Lan laughed, then said bye and started skiing. Lan loved it. This was absolutely ridiculous. Legal advisor? Life just seemed to keep getting better. A raven flew over his head and as it cawed Lan had a thought: *embrace the trickster.*

Halfway down a slope, Lan caught sight of a man farther up on a ridge, just above one of the most dangerous cliffs in this area. Lan had never seen anyone hit it, and couldn't believe this guy thought he could.

Lan watched with both awe and fear — the man jumped, at full speed, stylishly landing in deep snow thirty feet away like it was no big deal.

Lan shook his head and then blinked. It was the big foreign guy, the same one from the shack with wooden skis. Lan took after him, determined to catch up. He absorbed every bump while trying to keep focus, but he couldn't gain on him.

Then, just as Lan blasted through some trees, he came face to face with the man he pursued. Lan slammed on the brakes to avoid hitting him. The massive man was standing there, waiting for him, smiling through his thick beard.

He bellowed, "I knew I would find you!"

Lan was still out of breath, but managed to gasp, "Me? I was coming after you!"

The man laughed. "I have something for you." He then took off on his old wooden skis.

Lan couldn't hold back his enthusiasm. "I can't believe you sent it off that cliff back there! That was huge! I have always thought about hitting that."

The man stopped and then called back. "Now you've seen it you can do it yourself."

Lan shook his head and laughed. He couldn't believe this dude. "Uh, you said you have something for me?" Lan thought of the drink he had given him last time.

The man shook his head. "Yes. Something that will help you ski better. Well, do everything better. Help you understand the *deeper* side of things better."

Lan was now more confused. "Okay ... what is it?"

The man's expression was unreadable. "Come over here."

Lan shrugged, then slid over to him. He was standing near the massive crystal near the base, the mysterious rock that no one could explain.

The man spoke to him. "What is it you care most about in the world?"

Lan laughed nervously — that was a strange question. But he was curious, and felt oddly excited, so he played along.

"Hmmm. What do I care most about in the world? Yeah, man, well, I guess ... winter, right? But I dunno, lots of things. The earth, snow, skiing, girls, friends, family, all pretty high on the list." Lan then thought for a moment. "Sorry, I don't know, that's probably too many answers."

"Those are great answers." The man then reached into his pocket with his giant mitten. His beard, his blue eyes, his massive hat, his wooden skis, everything about this guy seemed so otherworldly. Lan then noticed something he hadn't previously: were those horns coming out of his hat?

When Lan saw what he pulled out of his pocket though, everything felt even weirder and time seemed to stop. Lan wasn't sure what he was looking at, but he couldn't deny some immediate attraction to it. He looked closer and reached out to grab it. It was a bracelet of sorts, not a full circle, but open enough for someone to put it around their wrist.

"You are giving this to me?" Lan asked, studying it with reverence.

"I think you should have it. I am sorry to wrap you in this whole situation. But this is exactly what has to happen." The man said this eerily, and Lan laughed nervously again.

"Situation?"

"Oh, never mind. It's a gift. Are you ready?"

"Alright, man, whatever. Thank you?"

The man then grabbed the bracelet back from Lan and the storm suddenly picked up. Lan glanced around and felt like the energy had just gotten really creepy. He looked back at his new companion. His deep blue eyes suddenly brought an intensity of fear to the situation. The man wasn't joking at all. He was dead serious.

The man spoke. "Do you, Lan, Ian Winters of Colorado, swear on all that is holy to you, the earth, snow, skiing, girls, friends, family, and winter, to protect this arm ring at all costs? Do you swear an oath that you will not take this arm ring off until you return it to its rightful owner?"

How did he know my name? Lan thought, wondering if he should panic. The storm had only gotten stronger, and though he couldn't see well he felt like there was a strange light emanating from the crystal. He looked back to the massive, crazy man and choked out ... "Um, what? An oath? I guess?"

"That's not how you make an oath," the man replied, looking for the first time very impatient. "Say it aloud."

"Oh," Lan muttered. "Okay, sorry. I swear on all that is holy to me," Lan then repeated despite freaking out, "to protect this arm ring at all costs, I swear an oath to Ullr of Asgard, to not take this arm ring off until I return it to its rightful owner."

Lan didn't know where those words even came from. Ullr? Wasn't that the name of that alcohol? Were they actually connected?

The massive man suddenly pulled out a knife.

Lan really panicked now. "Uh, oh shit — what?"

"Just blood," the man grunted, then quickly slashed Lan's palm. He then smeared the blood across the bracelet and put it on Lan's wrist.

The storm calmed suddenly, but Lan felt incredible. Maybe it was the adrenaline, but he looked at the bracelet now on his wrist and wondered if it had something to do with this feeling. He couldn't tell what it was actually made out of. It wasn't steel; maybe wood, but really hard? Like petrified wood, polished, but it still looked somehow fresh like there was still bark on it, and there were etchings running across it.

"Thank you," the man said to Lan, sighing like he had been released from a burden. "Don't tell anyone. Especially not on that social media thing you people use." The man then slapped Lan hard on the back and skied off.

Lan yelled after him. "Wait, what? How do you know my name? Where are you going?"

The man didn't reply — he was gone.

"Ullr?" Lan said, speaking the strange name that had just come to him during the oath.

He looked down at the armband and then at his bleeding hand which, surprisingly, seemed fine. Lan felt confused, but he also felt somehow ... connected. He then gazed out into the forest and there it was, the tree from the other night, its branches and roots somehow intertwined with his veins and arteries. He once again felt like he had on that fateful night, the first time he met the big man.

"Lan?" A woman's voice suddenly called through the trees. He looked up. Linnea was skiing towards him.

"Who was that you were talking to? He was so tall!" She exclaimed.

Sasha had been on the phone way too much recently. It seemed to run his life. He missed the simple days when all he cared about was skiing. Being in Teton Hole kept reminding him of that one season, the one after college, when he was worry-free. His work now consumed his free time, but he was so close to achieving great things in the tech world. He just needed to meet the right people. He knew that technology could help save the world, and he wanted to be a part of it.

He put the phone down for a second and considered how his obsessive ambition was starting to wear on him. The eviction was stressing him out, and it didn't help that he hadn't been sleeping well.

He took a deep breath.

Even though he had started praying regularly, the nightmares just wouldn't stop. Every night he would dream of the demonic man coming to take his land. Every night he would jerk awake, feeling guilty about owning land, which then led him to feel guilty about evicting the skids from the Brown House. He couldn't help but think the dream had something to do with the eviction, and after the so-called legal advisor showed up, it was too much to handle.

He had decided to give the skids more time, hoping that would free him from the possessive nightmares. But no: once again he awoke full of fear.

If Sasha hadn't been so worn out the next morning, he might have had the foresight not to answer his dad's phone call. He didn't tell his father about the dream. He didn't want to sound crazy, but his father stressed him out anyway. He was upset because Sasha didn't seem to give any reason for putting the eviction on hold; instead of sounding crazy, he sounded incompetent. His father was offering him this opportunity to make some serious money off the house he had bought him, and he had blown it.

His father's lawyer then called him. Despite his initial frustration with this situation, Sasha found the lawyer to be quite charming and, in fact, very optimistic. Something about his voice seemed to put him at ease. They chatted for a long time, discussing a number of topics, and then the lawyer mentioned that he knew someone in the tech field and would connect them. Also, the lawyer would be in Teton Hole in a few days and suggested they meet up. They would turn this whole thing around.

That night, Sasha slept like a baby, with no nightmares. Maybe he had just been too stressed out recently? Feeling on a roll, Sasha reached out to the investors the lawyer had connected him to. They loved his perspective and wanted him to trial some new and innovative technology before it went on the market — "a miracle technology." He couldn't believe it. He felt immense pride, his connections were finally paying off. Were his prayers finally being answered? Postponing the eviction was apparently the perfect move.

A few restful days later he opened the package excitedly — Christmas had come late. He tore through the bubble wrap and pulled the rectangular-shaped device out of the plastic covering. For all the build-up it was actually a pretty simple thing; a monolithic black box that looked a bit like a hard drive with the company name, Nanotech Industries, engraved on it.

Sasha held it in his hand with a look of wonder and thought to himself, *the future is here.* The instructions said to plug it into the phone and go from there. He did so. A voice immediately started speaking from his phone.

"Thank you for using the groundbreaking new technology from Nanotech Industries. You are helping to make the world a better place. We hope you enjoy it. Please fill out the survey daily so we can receive your feedback. To begin, please place your thumb upon the fingerprint reader so we can create your new digital identity."

Sasha did as he was told, then felt a sudden sharp pain. He pulled his thumb back and noticed a small amount of blood coming out of it.

He sucked on it while the voice continued: "Thank you, Sasha. We have confirmed your identity and your account has been created. We look forward to your feedback."

Sasha stared at the screen, a bit baffled, expecting something else to happen. The app opened a feedback survey, but his only feedback thus far was that he suddenly had a bad headache.

"So," Lan asked in awe, "there's also a big Swedish woman around town? They must be related?"

Linnea shrugged. "Maybe. I'm not sure she is Swedish. Scandinavian at least. What did he say to you?"

Lan answered, looking a bit confused. "Oh, I dunno, I saw him send it off this huge cliff, but we had met a couple of weeks ago in a shack, and then we were just kind of talking — it's hard to explain." Lan then grabbed his wrist, looked at his hand in confusion, and then suddenly hugged Linnea.

"Sorry," he said, letting go of her. "It just feels so weird and right. Like, I finish talking to this crazy guy and then you show up out of nowhere and start talking about how you have met some woman who looks very similar to him."

Linnea laughed and looked at Lan. He was covered in snow and smiling. He looked both adorable and silly and she suddenly wasn't sure what she was feeling. Then, surprising herself, she asked him, "Do you want to come over for dinner tonight?"

"Me? You are inviting me, your real-life friend?" He stepped towards her and gave her a little nudge with his elbow. She nodded shyly.

Linnea was excited to show off her cooking skills, but as she later looked through the fridge she realized she might need to go shopping. She only had one meal left to make and needed to use that stuff before it went bad. *Should I just make it? Why not?*

She texted him just in case. "Does Mexican food work for you? Tacos?" And she smiled at his response: "Does it ever!"

She told her roommate Sylvia that he was coming over. "Like tonight? Soon?" Sylvia asked, excitedly.

"Yeah, tonight. We ran into each other and I don't know what got into me. I invited him over. Do you think it's too much?"

Sylvia laughed. "Not the way you look when you talk about it. I guess I will get dressed and find something to do out in the world."

"What?" Linna got suddenly worried. "No! You have to stay and eat, there is enough food for sure and, this way, you can actually tell me what you think about him."

"Okay, fine, but I'm only hanging out for food and then I'm running to my room to turn on a loud movie!"

"Oh, stop it." Linnea blushed.

At dinner, Silvia did a lot of the talking, just as Linnea had hoped. "So Lan ... or, I mean, is that what you prefer to be called?" Sylvia asked.

"It's whatever you want," he said with a smile.

"Ok, whatever, I think it's funny. Sir Lancelot! So what do you do when you're not skiing? Linnea said you read a lot?"

Lan replied quickly. "Yeah, I read all kinds of things, but mostly been reading sci-fi and mythology lately."

Silvia bubbled. "No way! I love sci-fi, but I lean harder into the fantasy."

"Oh, anything fantasy is also my jam. "*The Lord of the Rings* is my original love."

Linnea liked watching him talk to Sylvia. He was funny and easygoing and he wasn't awkward around other people. Also, Lan wouldn't stop exclaiming how delicious the dinner was. He seemed almost overly happy, which kind of scared Linnea in a sense, mostly because she felt the same way.

He seemed a bit different than the other night. He hadn't wanted any wine, which seemed odd. Maybe he was just nervous like she was, but that made her want wine.

"You two have fun!" Sylvia said, standing up from the table. She then shut the door to her room, flaunting two big thumbs up and a smile.

Linnea had hoped she might stick around a little longer.

Lan got up too, and then started playing tug of war with Bailey in the living room. Linnea was impressed — he was really good with her dog.

"Sylvia is super cool," Lan said, looking up from his struggle with Bailey.

"Oh yeah, I know, we have a lot of fun as roommates."

"Yeah, so do I and my roommates," he said. She thought he looked like he was going to say something more, but then he didn't.

She spoke instead. "I liked — I mean, I still like — hanging out with you."

He grinned at her. "Me too."

Then they were both silent for a little too long to be just a pause. It didn't feel awkward to Linnea, though. It felt almost energetic.

He moved closer to her and said, finally: "maybe we save more talking for later?"

She nodded, and then let herself go, surprising herself with some of the things she just naturally did. For a moment she thought she was losing control, but then suddenly realized it was the opposite — she was taking control.

After some time on the couch, they moved towards the bedroom. Afterward, quite some time afterward, Linnea snuggled up next to him. Hearing how loud Sylvia had turned up her volume, Linnea blushed.

Lan had put his arm around her and pulled her close. She reached out and grabbed his other hand, and then looked at the bracelet on his wrist.

"This is neat. Where did you get it?"

Lan laughed more than she expected. "Well, you aren't going to believe this, or maybe *you* will, but the giant foreign guy gave it to me earlier."

She fondled the bracelet in her hand for a moment and suddenly felt a healing force rush through her, an emotion so overwhelming that she could only describe it as love. This was both exciting and terrifying. *I can't be in love already,* she wondered to herself. *Or could I?*

The moon was very small, its silvery crescent cutting through the break in the clouds like a scythe as Lan and Pierce walked towards downtown. Lan was trying to explain to Pierce how phenomenal he felt. How he had had an amazing couple of days, how felt like he could do anything. Something was just different, like *inside* of him. He had this sense of wonder about the world which he had never really experienced. He would stop and look at the smallest of things for minutes, creating a little story about everything. And the trees — he was suddenly obsessed with trees. He felt almost like a tree himself, grounded, centered, and focused.

"Yeah, dude." Pierce laughed. "It's a cool fucking tree. I am fucking starving, let's go eat."

"Yeah, yeah. Sorry," Lan answered. "I'm just, I don't know, stoked."

"I know. You've told me like a million times, dude. Ever since you started hanging out with this chick, you're all googly-eyed about everything."

They walked into the restaurant. Lan stood in line as Pierce talked to people he knew, which was basically everyone. Lan fiddled with the new bracelet he had received the other day, reveling in the magic of the moment when he said an oath to it.

Lan hardly felt like drinking. Ever since he had stayed with Linnea, he didn't feel like drinking at all. But he bought Pierce a beer and, feeling generous, also bought his pizza.

"Lan Rover? Big Papa P? Is that you guys?" Chelsea was yelling across the restaurant at them. Linnea, her roommate, and another girl he didn't recognize were with her. They came over to join them, and Lan watched with hypnotized wonder.

Linnea looked magnificent. Her dark long brown hair was braided, she wore a black top, and a bluish quartz crystal hung right where Lan wasn't supposed to look. But, was it glowing?

"Yay!" cried the girl Lan didn't recognize. "This is so great! Just gonna do a quick story!" She then pulled out her phone and began pointing it around the group. The girls all shouted "woo" at the screen, and when it was Lan's and Pierce's turn to be filmed they both put their hands up. Lan's sleeves were slightly pulled up and he flashed a metal sign. Afterward, Lan noticed his bracelet was exposed, so he pulled his sleeves back down nervously. Fear shot through him. Hadn't the big man warned him about social media?

The guys watched the women walk over to the line, and then Pierce said, "Good work, Lan. I'll be right back, I'm taking a leak." Pierce set his phone down and walked off.

Lan looked at his own phone and saw that Couch Guy had texted that he was on the way. Lan then closed it and looked around. He suddenly noticed a man standing at the bar looking really out of place. He wore a suit, his hair was slicked back, and he was talking loudly.

Lan found himself staring at the guy. Something about the way he spoke and the way he looked was just strange. Was this guy a billionaire? At this place? He looked somehow fiery and menacing.

As if he could tell he was being stared at, the man stopped talking and looked straight at Lan. Lan quickly looked away, but suddenly felt very hot and light-headed.

"Hi, Lan!" Linnea had just appeared next to him. He awkwardly hugged her from his chair and then looked for the man again. He was gone.

"Are you okay?" she asked. "You look a little pale."

"Yeah," he started. "I'm fine."

Lan began to get up as Pierce's phone buzzed. He looked down at it and noticed a face on the screen, a very familiar face. Oddly, it was almost as if the face were looking out of the screen directly at Lan. His body tensed immediately when he realized it was the same guy who had just been at the bar.

Lan continued watching, ignoring Linnea. The man on the video — but was it really a video? — pointed to his own eye, and then pointed to Lan as if to say "I see you."

The screen then went black, and Lan jumped. He then pushed the phone across the table a bit too violently, and it slid off the table. He looked up and saw Linnea was looking at him with mild concern.

"You're just throwing my phone around, Lan?" Pierce accused, having just returned, picking it up off the ground.

"Sorry, bro. It did something weird," Lan answered, awkwardly.

"You're weird," Pierce replied.

"Pierce!" Linnea said excitedly. "I heard you guys have had a victory in the eviction situation?"

"Yeah, I mean —" Pierce started. "I just couldn't put up with the way the landlord was treating us, y'know? I had to do something."

Linnea laughed and gave Lan a knowing look. As if on cue, Chelsea called out as Couch Guy came in. "Here comes the hero of the house!" She ran over and gave him a hug.

They all ate pizza, and most of them drank. Lan kept staring at Pierce's beer and wondering why the idea of drinking seemed so strange to him recently. That feeling of spirit in everything seemed to be echoing out of Pierce's beer, and not in the best way: it was mildly dark and ominous.

Linnea was talking with her girlfriends, and Lan was having a hard time focusing in general. Everyone was talking so loudly and he felt he couldn't concentrate. Something had ungrounded him.

Who was that guy at the bar a minute ago? And did he really just show up on Pierce's phone? *I'm not any higher than usual,* Lan thought to himself.

As the crew all made their way upstairs to the music, Lan tried to get Linnea's attention, hoping to maybe have a minute to talk with her. But she was talking intensely with Sylvia and he didn't want to interrupt.

The show was packed. It seemed everybody had come out for New Year's Eve, and the lines at the bar became insane. Lan talked a bit with Couch Guy and Pierce but then decided to go to try to dance with Linnea. The women were all dancing together, and Linnea didn't even seem to notice him at all. He would dance by her, and then try to dance with her, but she seemed to just ignore him.

Maybe I should just get a drink, he decided, frustrated. He left the dance floor and stood in the absurd line. Waiting, and then waiting more, he looked around wondering what he was even doing here.

He felt suddenly annoyed. He had felt so good recently, and he hadn't been drinking at all. He was so excited about Linnea and felt like she would help him be a better person. But *she* was certainly drinking tonight.

He had to fight for the bartender's attention but with little success. He instead glanced across to the other end of the bar. To his amazement, sitting opposite of him, chatting happily, was the guy in the business suit he had just seen downstairs. *What the fuck is going on?* Lan wondered. *Who is this guy?*

Lan stared at him some more, but then the bartender asked what he wanted. He glanced back over at the businessman and noticed that the person he was talking to looked familiar.

No, he thought. *I know that guy.* Lan was baffled — the man was talking to his landlord, Sasha.

One of Lan's co-workers came up behind him and started talking to him, using Lan as a cover for cutting the line. Lan chatted for a moment, then looked back. Both the strange man and his landlord were gone.

Beer in hand, Lan then went back to the dance floor. He tried to feel excited, but he suddenly felt like everything had gotten dark and even a bit scary. Worse, Linnea continued to avoid him.

As he stood in the back corner, wondering what was happening, he realized the beer was not doing it for him. He took a few sips and felt like he was immediately sucked back into the frustration of the last month. The drinking had been a way to cope with the unknowing surrounding the eviction. A strange feeling told him that the booze had been possessing him.

"Hey!" he said to Linnea. "Sorry! I gotta leave!"

"You're leaving?"

"I mean, I guess." He had to shout because of the loud music. "You want to come chat for a second?"

She followed him outside, and he said, "You just don't even seem that excited to dance with me."

"You just want to talk every time we dance!" She continued, "I just ... well ... do I have to give you all my constant attention?"

Lan was baffled. "No, I didn't say you did!"

"Look, Lan, I don't know, sorry. Everything is just moving so quickly between us and I am just freaking out a little bit. Can we just maybe slow things down a little?"

Lan replied reactively, "We don't have to move so quickly, I didn't think we were moving too quickly! But also there is no pressure. Really!"

All Linnea said was, "Thanks for understanding," and then went back inside.

He felt crushed. Lan rolled a cigarette, lit it, and started walking down the alley towards his house. How had everything just gone from being incredible and wonderful to being dark and terrible? Shadows loomed around every corner, and his mental state teetered on total destruction. He didn't think he was pressuring Linnea to do anything too quickly, but she seemed to think so.

He suddenly heard a noise: the loud cawing of nearby crows. Lan breathed out smoke, then looked around him. There certainly seemed to be a lot of crows — or were they ravens? — on this block. The fence on either side was lined with them, cawing as he walked past them. Some took flight and landed on the ground in front of him, and a few others swooped down from higher perches over his head. He loved ravens, but these ones were kind of freaking him out.

Someone walked out of the shadows in front of him. The ravens responded, moving out of his way and screeching some more. Lan walked to the far right side of the alley, hoping to avoid too much contact. It was an old man, limping towards him, wearing a wide hat. Lan tried for the standard small-town head nod as he got closer, but the man suddenly lunged, grabbing Lan's shoulder with a really tight grip.

He then said, only, "The future is coming for you," before letting go and walking past him.

Lan couldn't move, even though the man was now well behind him. He kept thinking about his face like there was something wrong with one of his eyes. And, just then, all the birds took flight at once in a cacophony of shrieks.

Lan turned to look behind him. The man was gone.

Linnea snuggled up against Bailey in the late morning. Her head was pounding even though she wasn't moving. "Why do I do this to myself?" Linnea said aloud. "What a great way to start the new year — hungover."

Linnea felt terrible about a lot of things. She hadn't told Lan, but her ex-boyfriend had been at the show last night. Sure, they only dated for a year, but it was long enough for everything to be weird. She didn't mean to be so distant towards Lan, but seeing her ex — along with old friends she hung out with when they dated — was too much.

She texted Lan. "Hey, sorry about being weird last night. I can explain. Feel terrible today but can we maybe chat tomorrow, (when I feel better) to clear some things up? Hope you don't feel too bad yourself."

She pulled Bailey closer. She then looked at the photo which Lan had given her the other day. It was a breathtaking shot of the Tetons with the red hills in front of them, but she mostly liked the note which came with it: "From: your real-life friend."

Sure, she had been feeling at times that things were moving too fast, but expressing it so harshly last night wasn't exactly how she wanted to deal with it.

She took Bailey for a walk. Being outside certainly helped, but as she looked at the grey skies, she realized how much she missed the sun. It had hardly been out in the last month with so much snow.

When she returned, she saw that Lan had replied. "All good :)" His dumb phone emojis made her smile. His text continued. "And sounds good, hit me up tomorrow."

She drove out to the ski village once it got dark. She rarely drove out there, but parking was free at night and she wanted to have her own car. She brought the blue crystal she had found — or had the strange woman meant it as a gift? It was so peculiar that the plans they had made were just "meet here at this time" rather than a text. Without texting, you have to stick to the plan you make. If you bail, people will worry about you not showing up. Phones make it easy to be flaky.

The village felt empty. No one was around, and nothing was open. The lights of the groomers illuminated the hill and Christmas lights lit up the base, but otherwise, things felt a little desolate. It had snowed lightly in town, but out here at the resort the snow was really coming down. Linnea brought a headlamp, and she had to put on skis to get to the massive crystal because it was a little way up the hill.

She was a minute early according to her phone. She wanted to check messages, but the screen was getting too wet. Her phone screen suddenly turned a bright white, and Linnea hit it a few times, worried something had happened.

The wind picked up, and she shivered. She turned off her phone, and as her eyes adjusted to the dark she noticed that the crystal did seem to emanate its own light, just like the one she found. She heard a cracking sound, so she turned around just in time to see the strange woman coming, skiing, with the large wolf running behind her.

Linnea stared in awe through the dim light. The woman was wearing a different cloak, this one with beautiful patterns and swirls. Her hair had some sort of iron cuffs that held her braids together in front, but it also fell loosely behind her and seemed to almost shimmer a whitish-blue in the crystal light. She also wore blue lipstick, which made her face look even more pale. And she was wearing something on her head, something like a wooden crown.

"I am glad you came," the large woman said softly.

Linnea smiled. "Thanks again for inviting me!"

The woman took off her skis while Linnea walked over to the giant crystal. "Oh, I brought this!" Linnea said and then pulled out the woman's crystal.

The woman wasn't smiling as much as before. In fact, she seemed very, very serious, more serious than Linnea was used to from anyone. She reached out her hand, grabbed the crystal from Linnea, and then placed it on top of the long, intricately carved stick she was holding in her other hand.

Linnea blinked in disbelief. Lights seemed to suddenly flicker around the woman like candle flames.

"No way," Linnea blurted out. "You really are a witch, aren't you?" Linnea then fell quiet, noticing the expressionless way the woman stared back at her.

Finally, the woman smiled and took off her cloak. She put it down on the ground near the base of the stone, and said, "Sit with me."

Linnea sat down across from the woman and watched as she tossed a bag of rocks in between them.

"Have you ever read the runes, Linnea?"

"Runes? Uh, no. But it's a form of divination, right? Like Tarot?"

The woman nodded and continued. "It is similar to Tarot, but much older." Then, straightening her posture, she added, "Pull a rune."

Linnea started to reach for the stones and then asked, "But don't we need a question to ask the runes?"

"All questions are really the same question: what does the future hold?"

Linnea shivered again. She shook the bag, listened to the stones tap against each other, and reached in.

"What does the future hold?" she asked aloud, then pulled out a rock etched with a simple symbol — a line, like an uppercase "I," or a lowercase "L."

"*Isa*. The rune of ice." The woman said. "A great storm is coming."

Linnea laughed as the snow continued falling. "Well that's nothing new, the great storm hasn't stopped."

The woman didn't laugh. "This storm will be different."

This silenced Linnea completely. She felt embarrassed as she connected the dots.

"*Fimbulwinter*." She whispered.

"I will pull one now," the woman said as she put the other rune back, shook the bag, and pulled a stone with purpose. She dropped it between them, and it rolled against the candle.

"*Kenaz*. The rune of fire..." The woman's eyes widened as she said this, and then she cleared her throat.

"What does that mean?" Linnea asked curiously, trying to contain her excitement and act serious, too.

The woman attempted to clear her throat again but she started coughing. Just like the other day, it was a deep and aggressive cough.

This all had suddenly become less fun. Linnea wanted to help but didn't know what to do. Finally, after what seemed like far too long, the woman stopped, her eyes watering, and she spoke: "A weapon will be used."

Linnea felt worried. "A weapon? Hey, are you ok?"

The woman put the stone back in the bag and shook it once more, ignoring the question. "And now the spirits will choose a rune." She placed the bag between them and Linnea waited in anticipation, wondering if she had heard correctly.

Linnea asked, "What spirits?"

At that moment a huge gust of wind moved through the circle. Linnea swayed with it in mild amazement. When she looked back down, she noticed the bag of runes had fallen over and one had fallen out. The symbol upon it was strange, like a tent symbol on its side.

"*Thurisaz* ... Jötunn."

"What is that one?"

"Giants." The woman said.

"Giants?" Linnea asked in bewilderment.

"The thorn, the *Jötunn are coming*. I ... I need to know more." The woman then said, "Breathe with me, Linnea, and find your inner sight."

Linnea didn't understand. "Ok ... But how did you know my name? I still don't know yours."

"I am Skaði, though this name means little to you yet. Now breathe with me. We must do Seiðr."

Skaði, Linnea thought. What a beautiful name. Linnea closed her eyes, feeling relaxed, perplexed, and excited all at the same time. After a few minutes, she was amazed to hear that the woman had started singing. Linnea opened her eyes for a quick moment. Reality seemed like a dream.

Whatever language Skaði sang in, it was beautiful but also mildly haunting. As she meditated, Linnea was still having thoughts, but it was as if a light was turned off by the singing. The thoughts weren't visible anymore. The singing was all there was. It felt like heaven, or something like it.

Out of the darkness behind her eyelids, an image appeared. It was hard to make out at first, like a frozen rainbow spread across a blank canvas. It was slowly getting bigger, or closer and closer. It was below her, and then it was gone.

Linnea was suddenly standing on a cold beach. She looked out and saw an impossibly large tree rising from the water. It grew and grew, and then soon it seemed to consume the sky, extending past the atmosphere, catching the stars between its branches like fairy lights.

A large splash suddenly disturbed her. Linnea looked to her side and saw the woman stepping into the water. She held her large stick — a staff — in one hand, and in the other, she held a large drinking horn. She shook the cup, and Linnea heard a rattle of stones — probably the runes.

The woman gave Linnea a weary look, and then bent over towards the water, filling the horn with it. She then stood upright again, walked back to the shore, and spoke: "I, Skaði of Jotunheim, ask the Norns to show me what they have written in the roots of the World Tree, Yggdrasil." And then she drank the water from the cup.

Linnea watched as something terrifying came over the woman. Her eyes had rolled back into her head, showing only their whites, and then she doubled over. The woman then fell into the sand, rolling on the ground as if in great pain. She flailed, shouting in an awful voice, "No, no, no!"

Linnea didn't know what to do. She looked around and saw there were three women standing in the distance watching both of them.

"Help us!" Linnea called to them. But the women, who looked very, very old, only looked back at Linnea without reaction.

Linnea began to hear noises in the distance, wailing — no, sirens, like on police cars or ambulances. Linnea couldn't tell where they were coming from. Scared, she looked back at Skaði, who had suddenly stopped seizing. She got to her knees, and then stood up, looking around herself with a look of fear and urgency.

"We must go," Skaði said.

"But wait!" Linnea said with confusion. "What is this place? What happened to you?

"Someone has tampered with the roots." She looked shaken up and upset. "It's as I suspected. He has rewritten Ragnarök," the woman said, not answering her question. "But I know what I must do."

Linnea suddenly lost all sense, and felt herself flying, or falling, past everything she had just seen, with sirens blaring behind her. She fell into darkness and then opened her eyes.

She was sitting on the snow in the same place she had been before. But there was no cloak under her, and the woman was gone. Only the blue crystal sat upon the snow where the woman had been.

Oh, what in the heck is life anyway? Lan wondered, stepping outside the Brown House to pee with Roscoe, the Couch Dog. The fog drifted down the street and surrounded the RV in the driveway. The morning air was crisp, a mystical frost covered everything.

As he peed, Lan noticed that tiny threads seemed to connect the landscape with a shimmering marvel. Everything seemed so alive! Even the RV had some life flowing out of it. He looked at the cotton-wood tree in the front yard and thought he could somehow feel its roots coming up through him. The tree — *to be rooted, but also be growing upwards.* Lan continued thinking. *Connected to your home, but still reaching out towards the sky.*

Lan felt intertwined with nature but disconnected from reality. In a realistic world, he'd have moved out by now. But nothing made sense in the actual world, because it is ruled by contradiction. As soon as everything seems too good to be true, something reminds you it's not.

The paradox suddenly moved through him, as if it came out of the ground, a message. *You need to write.* Lan returned inside with Roscoe and found himself writing in his journal. Couch Guy wasn't there, so he could actually sit on the couch.

> *The last few days I have had this feeling of confidence that over-whelmed me. I have felt so powerless the last however many years. No, I have been so pissed off. My fear seems to paralyze me. But the last few days, I have felt like, why abandon my own agency and blame everybody else? Why play the victim constantly?*

Lan looked up briefly at the beer cans scattered all over the table with a tinge of shame.

Suddenly Lan's phone buzzed. It was Linnea. She didn't seem mad at all. He went back to writing.

Lan looked away from the journal and at the arm ring. It seemed to pulse in a way as if connected to his heart, but it had a different rhythm. He wrote more:

That last word echoed through his mind as he looked over at the book sitting on the side table. It was the book about tricksters. He thought again about that strange old man with the weird eye, and all the birds, and what he said about the future coming for him. These strange characters in his life seemed almost like tricksters, and trickster energy can be intense — it isn't always good. He had invoked the trickster, hadn't he? He wrote one more thing.

Lan ran to grab his laptop, suddenly feeling the urge to look at that photo he had taken of this Ullr guy a couple of weeks ago. Lan searched through the photos on his hard drive. He stopped briefly and stared at the coyote he had taken a photo of. Something about its eyes made him shiver; it seemed to have something to do with all of this. He then clicked on the photo he had taken of the giant man.

The photo was still blank, overexposed, all white. Lan tried to play with the exposure on his editing software but nothing showed up. After staring, confused, at the screen for a while, he noticed the photo was slowly coming into focus. The man who looked like a Viking was now on the screen.

Lan saw the furs he was wearing, the old wooden skis. *Is this actually the god of skiing? Ullr?* Lan had a hard time believing he was actually a god, but he also had a hard time believing his own eyes.

Once the photo was in full focus it felt as if all rationality melted into oblivion. It seemed like the photo somehow came to life as if it had actually been a video. Snow was falling peacefully on screen.

Lan's face felt as if it had been absorbed into the scene. He then heard a voice, angry.

"You took a picture of me?"

The large man in the photo — or video — was now looking at Lan. Lan stared at his computer in mad confusion and then watched in terror as another person walked into the photo. It was the man in the business suit from last night, the one talking to his landlord.

The man had shown up on Pierce's phone, and now he was inside the computer. And then he spoke, but not to Lan.

"Ullr, you have become *níðing.*"

The Viking man slumped his shoulders, but instead of answering the man he looked out towards Lan and said, gruffly, "Thanks, *fífl.*" Lan didn't know what the word meant, but it didn't sound kind.

He continued watching as more people showed up in the photograph, other large men wearing strange clothes he couldn't understand. They looked like soldiers or security guards, but their clothes seemed too formal and too neat. They fell on Ullr, attacking him until he fell to the ground. Then, the men kicked him violently while Lan watched helplessly, pushing his face as close as possible to the screen.

Then, Lan jumped back, dropping his laptop. The man in the business suit was suddenly filling the screen and looking right at Lan, sneering.

"You are helpful, aren't you? You made this quite easy. I thought you didn't like technology?"

Lan cleared his throat, not sure what to say or believe. The man continued. "Did you ever consider that if you take a photo disrespectfully, Lan, you may be sucking the sacred out of your subject?"

He was smiling wickedly, and then he spoke one more time. "Better go answer the door."

Just as he said this, there was a knock on the front door of the house. Lan slammed his computer shut incredulously and slowly walked towards the door while Roscoe barked aggressively.

Lan pulled out his phone as he stared at the door in disbelief. He quickly texted Linnea: "Hey, I think I really need to talk to you. I may be in danger."

The knock came again. He pushed Roscoe out of the way and opened the door.

"Oh hey, Lan right?" It was his landlord.

"You are just the person I'm looking for."

PART 3: LOCAL AREA NETWORK

Lan looked through the door at his landlord, Sasha, in disbelief. Behind the man, the fog was still thick outside, and Lan noticed the cyber truck parked out on the street.

Lan's heart pounded in his chest as he stepped out and closed the door behind him, leaving Roscoe inside because they weren't supposed to have a dog.

Lan was nervous and cold. He should have put on a jacket.

The fog seemed to envelop the both of them as Lan joined the landlord on the front porch. "How's it going?" Lan asked, shivering as he reached out his hand.

The landlord acted like he hadn't seen the offered handshake and then walked over to Couch Guy's RV with what looked like feigned interest. "Now, this is a real beauty," he said. "Does your legal advisor live in here?"

Shit, Lan thought to himself. "Hey — man, we really appreciate you giving us more time to get out of here."

"Well, Lan — I mean, that is what we are calling you, right?" Lan nodded slowly.

"Good. I'm glad this housing situation worked out for you guys for so long. But, when it's time to sell, you have to sell." Sasha grinned.

Lan tried to read the expression on the man's face, and then said, "I, uh, guess so?"

Lan noticed something hanging from Sasha's neck. It was a silver cross. Sasha then reached into his coat pocket, producing from it a piece of paper. Handing it to Lan, he said, "You know, I am really glad your legal advisor came to me. Thought I should get my own legal advisor as well, so I did. And he pointed out that it's both clear in the lease and also state law that I'm fully within my rights."

Lan looked at the paper. It was a much more official eviction notice, stating they had thirty days to leave. Lan looked from it back to Sasha and then realized he was quite done with this conversation.

"Alright, well, fuck man, thanks for the extra time, I'm cold and it doesn't seem like there is much I can even do. I will tell Pierce."

Lan finished speaking but suddenly remembered that Sasha had said he wanted to talk to Lan specifically. He looked at him suspiciously. "Was there something else?"

"Well," Sasha said. "There is actually something you can do."

Lan furrowed his brows, suddenly wondering if the man was going to propose something sexual. But it ended up being something even stranger than that.

"I will tear this eviction notice up if you give me that bracelet on your wrist. I'll even give you a five-year lease."

Lan looked down at his hand. The sleeves of his sweatshirt had been rolled up, so they didn't cover the bracelet. But why in hell would his landlord want it?

Fear swept through him as Lan suddenly remembered something from the night before. Sasha had been at the bar, talking to the very same businessman who had just shown up on his computer.

"Wait, what?" Lan asked, bewildered.

"You heard me." Sasha looked at him with a fierceness Lan hadn't really expected. An air of violence hung between the two, and Lan stepped backward towards the door.

There is no way this is all connected, Lan thought, feeling a little crazy.

"I don't really know what you're talking about, man. This was a gift from my mom and I really can't just be giving it away. You could easily buy something better."

There was something weird going on with Sasha's eyes. They looked like they were twitching or even vibrating — there was something not right about him.

"You are going to let this eviction happen just for the sake of a bracelet your mom gave you? What would your roommates think of that? So selfish," Sasha said, in a suddenly very flat voice.

"Look, man, I don't know. You are freaking me out a little. Can I just think on it for a day and give you a call later?" Lan started to reach for the door, but then his landlord grabbed his arm and jerked him away.

Lan turned and sputtered. He didn't know Sasha well, but this didn't seem like him at all — he seemed almost possessed. Then, Sasha did something even stranger. He lifted up his own jacket, revealing the handle of a pistol tucked into his waist.

"You *are* going to give me that bracelet, Lan."

Lan shivered as thoughts flashed through his head. Ullr had told him to keep it hidden and not to give it to anyone. But Ullr wasn't here, and if that video he saw was real, then he wouldn't be showing up any time soon. And now his landlord had a fucking gun.

Lan's heart was racing. There was nothing to do but take it off. He tried and then panicked. He pulled on it, and then yanked on it, but it just wouldn't move.

Sasha became even more impatient. "Would you stop fucking around? Give it to me."

Lan shouted back. "I'm not fucking around. I really can't get the thing off!"

"Let me see," Sasha said, then grabbed Lan's arm. With his other hand, he tried to pull the bracelet off, jerking it repeatedly. Lan's wrist started to hurt.

Lan had enough. "Get off of me, dude! This is basically assault!" Lan pushed him off. Sasha started to reach for the gun, and Lan yelled.

"Look, man! I don't fucking know! I can't take it off! I said a fucking oath or some shit!"

Sasha suddenly let go of the gun and stopped moving. His eyes glazed over, and he looked very unfocused. "You swore an oath?" he asked him, almost sadly.

"Uh, yeah. I didn't really know what I was doing, but I was told I had to before I could put it on."

Just then, a phone rang, loudly, from within Sasha's coat pocket. Sasha pulled it out and then looked at it. Suddenly, he smirked and put it to his ear. "Yeah. Did you get that?" Lan became even more confused when Sasha then handed him the phone and said, "It's actually for you."

Lan hesitated, but feeling like he had no other option, he grabbed the phone and said, "Hello?"

No one answered, so Lan held the phone away from his head. He then saw a face appear on the screen — the businessman from the bar the other night, the one who was just on his computer.

He spoke. "Hey there, Lan! An oath, huh? That is just brilliant. Anyway, good *hamingja*."

Lan suddenly felt a pain course through his hand, and he dropped the phone. He then looked at his hand — there was a drop of blood on his thumb, like he'd just been pricked.

The door of the house suddenly opened behind him. It was Pierce. And just a moment later Couch Guy stumbled out of his RV, rubbing his eyes, trying to light a joint. Roscoe then ran out of the house, past Pierce and Lan both, barking.

Pierce asked, "What's going on out here?"

Lan felt dizzy. He struggled to explain, then finally tried to point at the landlord. Then, he fell backward, right into Pierce.

Pierce caught him with a shout directed at the landlord. "What did you do to him?"

"Hey — I'm just here to deliver the new eviction notice. Not sure what happened — he got pale. Anyway, hope he is ok." Then, shrugging and turning to leave, he added, "The notice is delivered. Great renting to you guys. Good luck at your next place."

Linnea made coffee while staring through her windows into the thick fog. She would walk Bailey, but she wasn't ready yet. She needed some more time to think about what had happened — or if it had actually happened at all.

She took her coffee to the couch, sipping it after wrapping a warm blanket around herself. She thought of the night before: the strange candlelight, runes spilling over from the wind, the meditation, the singing, the rainbow, the water, the unfathomable tree. And then the terrifying vision of the woman convulsing on the ground.

It had all felt like a dream, but she didn't think her imagination could have created all that. Was it possible that instead of a dream she was in a trance? She had never really been in a trance before. That ceremony seemed to be something like a seance.

This woman was a witch, or Linnea was going crazy.

Linnea wished Sylvia were back so they could discuss this. Or even Lan. Part of her was terrified. Whatever had happened didn't seem all that good. Those old women watching in the distance, and the noises which sounded like police sirens, had made things feel urgent. But Linnea also felt a trill of excitement — could she really have been in a trance? And could she learn to do this herself? Could she be a witch, too?

Linnea's phone interrupted her thoughts. It was a text from Lan, but not the reply she was hoping for: "Hey, I think I really need to talk to you. I may be in danger."

Danger? Linnea jumped up from the couch. She called Lan, hoping to find out what this was about, but he didn't answer. She needed to walk Bailey anyway, so she dressed quickly and hurried out the door. She left with a peculiar feeling that something very strange was going on in the world, but she had no idea how she was wrapped up in it.

Bailey ran out the door with her and happily sniffed and peed oblivious to any other drama. The fog brought an eeriness to an already eerie situation, and the houses were barely visible from the street. She heard large birds, probably the many ravens she'd seen the last few days, flapping through the thick fog around her. Linnea walked fast, almost running. So many thoughts raced through her head, and she was overwhelmed.

As she approached the house she was surprised to see a cyber truck parked in front of it. She then jumped as a man in a large jacket walked out of the fog. She recovered and smiled lightly to say "hi," but the man ignored her and kept going. She walked closer, around the RV, and then stumbled into a very strange scene. Pierce was pulling someone into the front door of the house, while Couch Guy, obviously quite stoned, stood unhelpfully smoking a joint while reading a piece of paper aloud to no one in particular.

"Yeah. This one is legit. Thirty days!" He yelled and inhaled again.

Linna shouted. "Oh my god! Is that Lan?"

Pierce answered her. "He's fine. I think Lan just got a little light-headed, he seems conscious." Pierce then smacked Lan on the face a few times. "Lan, man, you ok? Are you there?"

Lan had started rolling around slightly, groaning as if he was sick. His hands were around his head. He then began to speak, but it all sounded like gibberish.

"Well, great," Pierce said. "Now he is speaking in tongues."

Lan suddenly stopped. His body relaxed, but his eyes still seemed to be moving under his eyelids. Linnea watched in horror, and then suddenly realized this all seemed familiar. The woman, Skaði, had done the same thing when she had gone into a trance. But this was different, though. He almost looked possessed.

Then, he suddenly opened his eyes with a jolt and looked at them "What just happened," he asked. "How did I get back inside?"

The darkness absorbed him as he woke. His eyes adjusted to the lack of light, and he rolled over to find more pain. Everything hurt.

He didn't feel like himself — he felt distant, trapped. If the last thing that he remembered was true, and he was actually online, he was now in a digital prison cell. But somehow, he could still feel pain.

A blinding light suddenly filled the strange room, and then came a piercing laugh. "Ullr, Ullr, Ullr — do you think you are some sort of god or something?"

Ullr grunted and moaned as he rolled over. His body ached and the light blinded him.

"Have you forgotten that there is only one God, Ullr?" The voice said bluntly. "I must say, I am disappointed in you. You've been reckless, ignorant, and just plain stupid. And now you're *nīðing*, a terrorist. A threat to the establishment, a force of chaos, an enemy of order itself." The man laughed again. "And tricking the kid into an oath to the Fateweaver? Really?"

Ullr tried to sit up against the wall behind him, straining to see his jailer. A man in a business suit smiled at him, eyes shimmering like candles in the dark.

"Loki," Ullr spat. "You can't touch him, you know what will happen if you do."

"Ah, of course I know. That's why I complimented you. Who would dare tamper with one of Ullr's mighty oaths?" His eyes blazed. "But when I'm done with him, he won't exactly be in the right mind to use the Fateweaver."

To Ullr, Loki's smooth words sounded of chaos and destruction. "You can't touch him!" he yelled.

"You really thought your scapegoat could actually avoid the power of the internet? Just because he doesn't have a 'smartphone?' Ullr —

you knew I would find him. I told you before — the machines don't care for prophecies. Machines make their own fate."

Ullr cursed. "I should never have trusted you." He grunted, unsure if he should have said that.

Loki laughed. "You trusted me? Really, after everything you know of me?" Loki shook his head, and something in his face suddenly changed. "Well, then, I'm sorry," he said, adding an almost imperceptible pause before adding, " ... for you. Welcome to the future, Ullr. It's time for you to give up your ideals and accept that technology is the only way forward. The Singularity is almost here."

A great grey castle rose out of a hillside, its many points piercing the toxic haze smothering the city. From its center jutted a tall skyscraper, the highest structure of all the city, while bland and repetitive buildings spread out beyond the castle walls.

The jarring contrast of old and new architecture gave Skaði pause. Especially, the modern buildings and endless shopping malls disgusted her. Was she really here? In Asgard?

Everything had changed in this place. Skaði hadn't been to the city for a very long time, but their informant (or was it an ally? She couldn't be sure) had passed along information on Her whereabouts. Skaði still didn't know if she could trust it, but her vision had shown this to be the path: save Her before Ullr.

She walked through the city streets, feeling eyes watching her from every direction. She'd hoped her disguise was enough. She had already broken the law, performing unsanctioned magic at the Well of Wyrd, so there wasn't any reason not to also shapeshift. She was Jötunn, and there was no turning back.

Skaði let her mind wander away from the fear and onto that young, eager human. Skaði hadn't intended on getting Linnea involved in any of this, but the girl had brought herself in and had sought Skaði out. The crystal had called to her, and she answered that call. Linnea now had a very important role in all this, by her own choice if not by her own foresight. Skaði smiled and mused: *Linnea will make a good Völva one day.*

Skaði's disguise seemed to work well enough for her to blend in unnoticed, walking through the streets that paved over the forest she had dearly loved. Everything had now become madness and very ugly. Vehicles clogged the roads as elves, dwarves, fairies, and all manner of other beings — previously dressed in enchanting finery but now stuffed into boring business suits — hurried down sidewalks to their drab offices. The closer she came to the castle, the more absurd the change became. Ancient buildings had been transformed into bureaucratic temples of The Order, and very little of what once was seemed to remain.

She was close to her destination now, and she thought again on the message from the informant. "I will provide the escape route, you just get her out. You will know the place when you see it."

At least on this last bit, the informant was reliable. This was absolutely the place, a new tower of corporate offices emblazoned with glowing letters on its otherwise bland facade: GREEN ENERGY FOR A CLEANER TOMORROW.

Skaði tried to contain her fury at its absurdity and then heard a nearby car speed and then crash into another car. It was far enough away that she knew she was in no danger from it, but it gave her a thought. This was a perfect example of both the madness of the city and of The Order: speed up until you crash. Skaði knew that moving like ice was a better solution. When things become too complicated, slow things down.

On the street corner, she breathed deep into her icy lungs, feeling the roots of the World Tree flow up through the concrete as she grounded herself, and then she entered the building. The guard at the desk barely seemed to even notice her: her disguise was working. She nodded to him, walked past, and then continued down a corridor. Further in, she saw someone looking even more official. She passed him, and then, when he was out of her sight, she shapeshifted again, matching her appearance to his. Skaði was now a prison guard. She would have no trouble finding Her now.

She walked through security, where, unexpectedly, she came upon a different kind of guard altogether. He looked at first to be wearing steel plate, but Skaði sensed no source of water within him, nothing to freeze. She then understood why. *Is it really possible?* She wondered. *They've started using machines as guards, too?*

She feared it would see through her disguise, but it hardly moved at all and Skaði continued past it. Now, she could begin to feel what she was looking for. She was closer, but her destination was deep below ground. She followed her intuition, found a flight of stairs, and descended for what felt like forever.

Finally, she reached the last landing and exited the stairwell. What she saw next worried her: another robot guard, this one blocking a large, heavy door. She couldn't shapeshift into this machine guard because its essence was too different: instead of spirit, it merely trilled with electricity.

But She was definitely behind that door — Skaði could feel Her. Skaði spoke, giving her voice as much authority as she could. "Here to transport a prisoner."

The guard gave no sign that it had even heard Skaði. She spoke again. "We're going to bring her upstairs. The Order requires her for something."

The robotic guard again made no sign. Skaði shrugged and then tried to walk past it to the door.

It suddenly came alive. "Return to your station. Protocol forbids contact or transport."

The voice spoke — if speaking is what the machine really did — with a strange digital coherency that almost sounded sarcastic. Skaði suddenly felt dumb. She had relied on things beyond reason thus far, and now she needed to reason with this robot.

Or not? "I'm well aware of protocol, you digital twat." Though there was no water in the machine, there was enough moisture in the air from the underground aquifer atop which the city had been built. Skaði called upon the ice and became the ice. Suddenly the walls began heaving and cracking with frost, and icy beams jutted through those cracks.

She quickly forced the guard up against the door with the massive icicles, then jumped back into the stairwell just before the machine exploded. Skaði waited for a breath or two, then exited, hoping to find that the explosion had destroyed the door.

It had, and she walked in cautiously. In the center of this cavernous room stood a massive machine and glass prison of pulsing energy. Inside it, there was a woman — skin dark as tree bark, with hair flowing and verdant — bound to a platform between jolting bolts of electricity.

Skaði suddenly understood. This was the "Green Energy" the signs through the city had advertised. There was nothing sustainable about it — they were harvesting Jörð's energy.

Skaði, in her natural form, searched for a way to open the door. She pounded upon the glass. "Jörð! I'm here for you!"

Very slowly the woman turned her head and looked at Skaði. Her eyes were rolled back in her head, the whites vibrating with electricity, but she spoke.

"It's okay, I'm okay. This is the only way. Leave me be, dear."

Skaði stared in horror at the tortured woman and said: "Fuck no, it's not." She then summoned down a huge icicle that fell from the heights of the cavern, plummeting directly into the lightning box. The electricity all transferred into the icicle and went directly up into the ground, neutralized.

The Goddess, the Giantess, Jörð — Earth herself — lay unconscious on the floor, barely radiating the energy of her own life. The woman moaned as Skaði caressed her face and spoke to her softly.

"Everything is going to be more than okay. I'm freeing you from Him." Skaði then picked up her old friend and hurried towards the stairs.

An alarm was now blaring and she didn't have long. Skaði climbed the stairs as if they were some great mountain, wishing the ascent would be her only difficulty. As she reached an upper level, a door blasted open violently. A mechanical guard with glowing red eyes stared at her. Its height matched her own, and its lack of soul made her shiver.

She tried to dodge it, but it grabbed her hair as she ran past. Jörð was now on the ground and Skaði was being lifted into the air by her neck. The monstrous machine seemed unfazed by her struggles and Skaði was losing consciousness.

As darkness closed in around her, she suddenly heard a loud crack and fell to the ground. A stalagmite of rock and earth was sticking through the robotic guard's chest. Skaði gasped for air and saw Jörð moving upon the ground, the faintest of smiles on her face. She still had some strength.

Skaði scrambled to pick Jörð back up again and continued up the stairs. An army of guards was waiting in the lobby. Skaði used the last of her energy to conjure two walls of ice from the ground, the sea of robots parting as she ran as fast as she could to the front door.

Skaði had never felt so relieved to see a vehicle in her life as she felt for the one waiting outside. Their ally had come through. They climbed into the strange-looking car and disappeared in plain sight. The Order had just lost something crucial. And Skaði was now a *nīðing*, just like Ullr.

Lan's head felt like it had been in a trash compactor. Linnea had helped him into his room so he could lie in his bed. She had done a couple of tests to see if he was concussed, but she said his eyes weren't dilated. He could also see fine, he could stand fine, and he hadn't actually hit his head. He felt perfectly normal besides his headache and memory loss, but she suggested they bring him in, anyway.

"I don't want to go to the hospital, just give me a minute," Lan said to her, a little irritated with her.

She snuggled up against him, attempting to comfort him as he tried to remember what had happened to him.

"I don't know. The landlord gave me the eviction notice and I can't remember anything that happened after that. I just woke up to you guys all staring at me."

"That's weird," Linnea responded. "Do you remember texting me this morning about how you thought you were in danger?" Linnea asked.

Lan didn't respond. He really could not remember. There seemed to be gaps in his memory — every time he tried to think too hard, his headache only worsened.

"I don't know, I don't remember saying anything about danger. Sorry, I just feel like shit. I thought I had only fainted, got light-headed or something, but this is lingering."

"Yeah, I don't know, either," Linnea said. "Whatever happened wasn't just you fainting, you were basically talking and rolling around. It was honestly pretty scary."

Lan didn't like hearing this. "I know! Look, I'm sorry, ok?" Lan barked back.

"You don't need to be sorry," she said. "I'm here for you. You just rest for a second, don't fall asleep, but just take some deep breaths and try to relax. I'm going to make you some tea."

When she left the room; Lan closed his eyes and took a breath. He felt so weird, and nothing made sense. The only facts he could wrap his head around were that he was actually getting evicted and that life in general seemed pretty shitty. He rubbed his temples, and then his whole head, hoping to ease the headache. As he massaged himself he realized there was something on his wrist. It was a bracelet. He looked at it in bewilderment. *Where did this come from?*

Linnea walked back in with the tea and spoke excitedly, "I wanted to tell you that I had the wildest time out at the village last night! You know that big Scandinavian woman I was telling you about?"

"Who?" Lan asked, blankly.

"You know, you met that random big Norse guy, and I met...."

Lan cut her off. "Hey, Linnea, do you know where I got this bracelet? Did you give it to me? I swear, my memory is just not normal right now."

Linnea suddenly looked pale, and then sat down on the bed next to him. She held his hand and looked into his eyes. She seemed really worried, which made Lan feel even more uncomfortable.

With a sad expression, Linnea spoke to him softly. "I didn't give it to you, no. Look, Lan, can we please just bring you into urgent care and get you checked out?"

"I'm fine!" he announced.

She leaned over and kissed him on the cheek. "Okay, I'm so sorry this happened to you."

Lan looked at her as she sat back up. Suddenly, he did remember something. "Hey, speaking of remembering things, didn't you say you wanted to tell me something today? Something about the other night, you said you could explain?"

Linnea responded after an awkward silence. "Well, yeah, I mean, that can probably wait until later, when you're feeling better and all."

"No," Lan said a little more aggressively than he meant to. "I want to know now, it was pretty weird how much you were avoiding me that night."

Linnea sighed. "Look, I'm really sorry I was acting that way. It was just that my ex was there and all of my old friends I used to hang out with when we dated."

"Your ex? Who is this? You haven't told me about your ex."

"It's nothing, Lan, I just didn't handle the situation well, ok? I'm sorry, I really do like you. As I said, sometimes it feels like things are moving a little too fast and that kind of freaks me out, but I just shouldn't have said it that night. I was mostly just scared of my ex seeing me with you."

Lan didn't like this explanation at all. "Didn't want him to see you with me? Clearly, you still have feelings for this guy if you are placing his emotions over mine, so fine." Lan was fired up.

Linnea went to respond but he continued. "No. You know what? I kind of just need to be alone right now. Thank you for the tea, but I already felt like everything was going to shit with the eviction and the fainting and now you tell me this, and I just can't right now. My head feels like it's going to explode."

Linnea stood up slowly with a face of shock. She looked like she might cry as she walked out the door, but Lan didn't care at that moment.

Pierce walked in just after Linnea left. "You doing alright, bud? Linnea just ran out — she looked upset. You wanna go ski or something?"

"Just leave me alone!" Lan yelled.

Pierce looked both confused and offended by this outburst but he shut the door. Lan lay there in a bit of a panic. What was going on? He didn't feel like himself, but who else could he be? His entire outlook on life seemed to have changed in a matter of minutes. He wanted to blame Linnea, or maybe the landlord, but the truth was that he was mostly mad at himself.

He felt like he had been a bit of an idiot recently, his life spiraling out of control, stuck in a shit show of ski bum shenanigans, paying no mind to his future. He had so much potential, and here he was, wasting it away.

He did remember one thing from the last few days: he had wanted to stop drinking so much. But now he also felt like he needed to change his whole life.

A new thought popped into his mind. *I need more money.* This thought seemed to ease his headache like a great burden had been taken off his shoulders. His random passions, skiing, photography, journaling, none of them made him any money. His idea that wealth can be redefined suddenly felt so ridiculous that he almost laughed out loud.

It's time to grow up.

He picked up his old flip phone and looked at it with disgust.

How immature had he been? His rebelliousness had gotten him nowhere, all he had done was make life harder for himself. He knew he was smarter than this. He just needed a big slap in the face, and somehow the real eviction notice had done this.

Lan found himself thinking about his buddy from college who had become a banker, and envy abruptly overwhelmed him. This guy had a family, went on tons of fun vacations, and seemed to be living the dream life. He kept posting things about picking himself up by his own bootstraps.

This is what Lan needed to do. He stood up quickly with reverence, feeling as if he was reborn: he was going to change his life. He was going to get a real job. He was going to be rich. He would buy his own land, go on vacations, and stop acting like an idiot. And especially, he would buy a new car — one of those electric ones, maybe even a cybertruck.

Skaði's glacial eyes filled with moisture as she peered out over the massive field. An icy tear slid down her face as pellets of snow swirled around her.

She looked with dread upon a great medieval wall rising out of the field like a dark force. Asgard lay behind those walls. Skaði was no longer allowed into the city without facing arrest for the crime she had committed.

She kept reminding herself this was what had to be done: this is what the runes had shown her. She accomplished her first task, rescuing Jörð. Now she would accomplish the second.

It was inevitable whenever you worked with the magic of the World Tree, Yggdrasil, you would have to make a sacrifice. She just had not immediately known when she started this journey that *she* would be that sacrifice.

She had no other idea how she was going to get Ullr out of his digital prison. Rescuing Jörð was within her abilities, but digital prisons were beyond her knowledge. The Order had stepped into new realms here. She had no way of entering that terrible place without possibly becoming trapped herself, and that would help no one. She would have to make a trade.

Skaði had left Jörð with Grandfather and had no clue where they had gone. So, if caught, Skaði couldn't tell them where Jörð was even if they tortured her. Only Fenrir would know.

She skied through the field toward the gates of Asgard in her crystal-studded furs, her white hair dancing chaotically in the polluted air. The giant woman felt small below the large gates, and she found herself doubting her actions.

Still, she needed to know Ullr was free. She took a deep breath and reminded herself: *Loki is on our side.*

With a piercing screech, the gates opened and a figure emerged from the massive doors. The man who approached wore a business suit, and his hair seemed to sizzle like burning coals that flared up with every gust. Skaði stood in the swirling snow, flaunting the blizzard that constantly accompanied her, patiently awaiting the fire. In the cold light of dusk, fire and ice converged upon the fields of Vígríðr.

"I commend your bravery, Skaði, but I am afraid it may not be for your benefit," Loki said, smiling.

"I am not here to discuss benefits with you, Loki," she said coldly.

"Well, I'm not here to do that, either. You know your crimes." A snowy swirl of wind wrapped around Loki as if she had summoned it towards him. He chuckled. "Should we discuss the weather, instead?"

"Just prove to me that he is free," she said, trying to restrain her frustration.

Loki then pulled a slim rectangular device from his pocket, like one of the human's phones. He held it up to her, and she looked into its screen. On it, she saw Ullr lying on the ground of a bleak-looking room, his body a heap of fur and blood. He looked terrible.

She then heard a robotic voice speak from off-screen. "Time to go." She watched Ullr look up in confusion as if he couldn't believe what was said.

The android spoke again. "Hurry up. We haven't got all day here."

Ullr slowly rose to a hunched standing position, clearly in a lot of pain. He walked out of the door cell and as he left the room his whole body de-materialized.

Skaði gasped.

"Where did he go? How do I know this is real?" Skaði demanded.

"Oh, it's real, my dear. And, of course, he is right back where he was when he got absorbed into the net."

On top of Grand Teton? Skaði wondered. She then took a deep breath and focused. She searched through the astral plane and looked for his spirit. She could see it. She could feel it. Ullr's spirit was free. The spirit of skiing had returned. She sent her message to him across the wind.

A tinge of sarcasm lining his voice, Loki said, "And now your end of the bargain would require that you come with me."

She narrowed her eyes and gave him a look she knew he would understand as violence.

"Make this easier for yourself," he said with a smile, his blazing eyes answering her challenge. "Do you remember that time, long ago, when the tides were turned? And you were the one imprisoning me?"

With a sigh which caused the wind to swirl violently around them both, Skaði started towards the gates. Loki laughed in shrieks as he fought for his balance, his hair violently flaming in the snowy draft. Ignoring him, she entered the gates.

Just within, she came upon someone she'd not seen for a very, very long time. She nodded to him and to the two ravens upon his shoulders. He nodded back, a gesture which somewhat comforted her. He must have seen her vision, as well.

With one last glance at the old man, she calmed herself, preparing for her punishment, her sacrifice. As her crown of horns was removed, a hood was placed over her head, the world around her went dark and she whispered to herself: *"There is no courage without fear."*

Linnea awoke with a gasp. She was covered in sweat and her room felt like a sauna. She opened the window to let in some cold air, but, to her shock, this hardly helped: it was warm outside as well. She laid back down and Bailey snuggled up against her. She tried to remember her dreams, but they seemed too distant now. All she knew was that they had been terrible.

She felt like Skaði was in trouble. Her own tears had been flowing a lot recently, and here they came again, streaming down her face in the dark of morning.

She lay in her bed and tried to think. Had Lan really just asked her to move to New York with him? Had he completely lost his mind? It seemed like it. He'd said he wanted to be closer to Wall Street, he wanted to be rich. He wanted to buy a Tesla. He wanted to own a mansion with solar panels. It didn't make any goddamn sense. Ever since the incident he had been acting really, really strange.

Linnea took a bath to help her relax and slowly watched the sunrise through her windows. It had felt like it had been months since she'd seen it, but now, in the last few weeks, it was there every morning shining brighter and warmer despite being in the wrong season. Still, she wrapped a towel around herself, then stepped outside to express her gratitude to it, a small ritual burning of incense to also cleanse herself.

The first hit of that vitamin D had certainly been welcomed by Linnea and all the others in town. But then it happened again, every day for a week, and then another, and then another. People started calling it "June-uary." Linnea had laughed along with this, but now found it to be no joking matter. It is too early for winter to be over.

These unseasonably warm weeks were some of the worst of Linnea's life. *This is why you don't get involved with people,* she kept saying to herself. Especially when you get excited, things will fall to pieces.

Linnea was a wreck, and it was mostly because of Lan. After she had told him she didn't want to move to New York, Lan told her he no longer wanted to hang out. He told her he had bigger plans for his life, didn't remember anything about meeting any giant Scandinavian people, and looked at her like she was crazy whenever she mentioned them.

She honestly did feel a little crazy. If Lan didn't remember them but she did, was it all just a figment of her own imagination? Was she becoming mildly schizophrenic? The games her mind seemed to play on her were getting quite scary, and she could reconcile none of it.

The only thing that anchored her reality was the fact that Lan still had the bracelet he had told her the Scandinavian guy gave him, and she still had the crystal Skaði had given her, so it all must have happened. She *knew* it had happened.

Lan had obviously texted her, telling her he was in danger, so maybe something had happened to him? Is it possible to wipe someone's memories? She kept thinking of the tiny vibration she noticed when she looked into his eyes, like something was inside of him or had taken him over.

It was warmer and warmer every day, and the last of the snow from the intense blizzards had long ago become slush. Despite this, Linnea, Chelsea, and Sylvia joined the many other people out on the slopes wearing goofy outfits and soaking up every bit of sunshine they could. And though they were there to have fun, Linnea found herself distracted. It was too warm.

Sylvia had noticed Linnea on the ski lift raising her goggles to wipe her eyes. "Oh Nea, are you crying again? I'm sorry honey, doesn't the sunshine help?"

"It does ... but I just can't stop thinking about Lan."

"Stop drifting into those thoughts," Sylvia said. "It's getting you nowhere."

Chelsea, who worked with Lan, added, "Dude, that guy has lost his marbles, I'm telling you. Forget him."

"I know," Linnea sighed. "It's not just Lan, though. I'm also worried about how warm it is. It kind of depresses me to think that it's only January and it's so hot. Is this how the future will be?"

Chelsea hugged her and said. "Let's just focus on things we can do something about. Fuck the dudes, fuck the future, let's just have fun!"

She handed Linnea a beer, and Linnea took a sip. She had been drinking more recently, and she knew it wasn't helping her emotional state.

"It's not all bad," Linnea added. "I got some crazy news at work last night. They want to make me a manager...." She said this with sarcastic joy, but she was actually really excited. To not be serving tables would be kind of wild. She would instead go around and do whatever it is managers do.

"No way, Linnea! Good for you! That is super exciting! A promotion? Will you make more money?" Sylvia asked.

Linnea smiled. "Yeah, I think so, I won't have to serve tables at least. Anyway, I just need to focus on the good things in life, right? I really appreciate you two being here for me the last few weeks.

"We are always here for you Linnea," both girls said in unison.

The skiing and friends did help, but Linnea still couldn't stop the dreadful feeling that winter was over. She had been so hopeful and excited during her experiences with Skaði, convinced that this so-called Fimbulwinter was coming. But now she couldn't stop thinking about that dream, the one where she was on top of the tram in the middle of winter and there was no snow at all.

35: The Land Of Burning Ground

Ullr stood upon the Grand Teton on a cloudless day, his antlers protruding into the sky majestically. He was in a confused stupor, squinting and sore, but once again feeling much more primal. He hadn't expected this. How long had he been in the digital prison? And why did they just let him out?

He shivered as he remembered the last moment in that terrible place. He had walked out of the cell room and looked down an endless hallway of open cell doors, each one with a robotic guard in front of it. What were they preparing for?

As he gazed out from atop the sacred mountain, a gust of wind suddenly blasted across the peak and a thought came to him: *find Fenrir in the land of burning ground.*

Skaði had sent him a message. She must have gotten him out somehow — but how? Suddenly, he realized how warm it had become and terror swept through him. Had Skaði traded herself for him? Ullr panicked: this would jeopardize everything.

He began his descent towards the east face of the Grand Teton. He allowed himself a smile, remembering the first time he'd skied this route guiding Bill Briggs down its slopes.

The top of the Grand was the easy part, besides the exposure. Ullr took big sweeping turns, managing the slough, but then, instead of the multiple rappels he could have done, he just sent it off some cliffs to the side. He flew through the air for at least several breaths, and let the adrenaline ease his sore body. He then shimmied his way through narrow couloirs and over jagged rocks. With his shield and bow upon his back, he found a state of pure focus. Focusing helped him ignore his fear.

By the time he reached the bottom, he was drenched in sweat and worry. What had Skaði done? She was the one who usually called him reckless, but she might have just sacrificed everything. Especially since Loki was proving that, yet again, he couldn't be trusted, ranting about the Singularity even more than before.

Ullr did all this to help Skaði, the love of his life, but now she had gotten herself captured, and likely for him. He knew he must do everything he could to help her.

She had sent Fenrir to the north, and Ullr would go that way. But first, he needed to see about the bearer of the Fateweaver. Ullr felt some guilt for this. He had roped the kid into something bigger than he could understand, and, worse, had put him in danger. He liked the kid, too — Ullr owed him at least an explanation.

He skied to the dwelling, a run-down house painted brown, trod past the large metal trailer that was also somehow a dwelling, and then knocked on the door. When the door opened, Ullr hardly recognized the man who stood in front of him.

Lan had cut his hair and combed it off to the side. His scraggly beard was now gone, replaced by a clean-shaven face that looked confused and upset.

"Can I help you?" Lan asked, no recognition coming through his expression.

Oh Gods, Ullr thought. *Loki has already got to him.*

Ullr wasn't sure what to say now. He stared at him for an awkward moment and Lan continued to stare back.

"Uh. Do I know you?" Lan asked.

Ullr's heart sank. "You really don't remember me?" Ullr tried.

"Sorry, man, you are kind of freaking me out."

Ullr sighed and looked into Lan's eyes. They vibrated in a way Ullr immediately recognized as wrong. Looking impatient, Lan pulled a phone out of his pocket. It was a smartphone.

Ullr cursed to himself. "Sorry about that, young lad, I was looking for someone else, I guess. I will let you get on with your day."

"Okay," Lan replied and, as he went to close the door, Ullr saw the arm ring was still upon his wrist. The Fateweaver was at least still safe.

"I will be back for you soon," Ullr said to the closed door, then turned to his long trek north.

The sun rose and set three times before he neared his destination; where the skies darkened with thick smoke. He'd come finally to the land of fire, the Land of Burning Ground as it was called until not long ago, the land of yellow stone as it was called now.

A great many spirits resided here, a great many peoples have worshipped this place, and a great many people were displaced from here. Ullr felt especially the absence of those people, those who'd been forced out. He could feel the ancestors of the land all around him, guiding him. In winter, it was harsh and hard to inhabit, but it reminded Ullr of home.

The clouds were black as charcoal and steam rose eerily from the ground. He skied past pools filled with fantastic blue-green water which boiled and stank. Great mud pots exploded all around him and geysers shot liquid fire hundreds of feet into the air.

Herds of elk and bison frequently approached him, showing their interest and recognizing his animality. He no longer needed to hide his antlers, and he happily traveled with a herd of elk for most of the day while ravens followed them overhead.

A long and lonesome howl broke the silence of his skis. Ullr looked to the east, listening as more wolves joined in. Birds shot up from the forest in immediate reaction to the chorus as the elk ran in the opposite direction. Ullr trudged into the deep dark woods, leaving the elk and ravens behind, in pursuit of those wolves.

After some thick bushwhacking, he searched the forest, seeking a sign, and found one. Someone paced between the trees, waiting for him.

"Oh, it's you!" Ullr said happily, greeting the coyote. "Have you seen Fenrir?" In response, the coyote then darted off deeper into the forest, and Ullr followed.

He continued to follow the coyote, but dusk was approaching quickly. Why wouldn't the coyote speak with him? Had something gone wrong? A second later a deep growl shook the forest around him. He shivered as someone came out of the shadows. A single wolf approached him. It was the biggest wolf of the forest, its jaws looking large enough to swallow the sun.

The large man stood his ground, but his nerves tingled. Suddenly the wolf pounced. Ullr closed his eyes as he fell backward, anticipating pain. Then, slobber ran down into his ears as the great beast stood above him, licking his face.

Ullr boomed a mighty laugh, then scratched the massive animal behind the ears and sat up. Fenrir began to whine and bark, and Ullr understood this as a sign to follow him.

Ullr skied behind the wolf through the black forest until they arrived at a cave. Ullr took off his skis and followed it into the darkness. He stumbled through the cold cave, occasionally catching the glint of the wolf's eyes up ahead. He felt briefly lost, but soon noticed a green glow in the dark of the cave, a faint light to which he made his way.

When Ullr found the source of the light, he entered and saw a circle of candles illuminating a naked old woman, her skin bracken, lying in a warm, steaming pool. Her hair floated around her, alight with energy, glowing green with streaks of grey splashed throughout.

She was bathing in the hot water, relaxed. Fenrir now stood by her side, and Ullr ran to her in awe. It was Jörð, the Goddess of the Earth, the mother of all, and especially of the Jötunn.

"Mother ... is it really you?"

The woman sat up, her dark wrinkled breasts floating in the water. "Ullr, it has been far too long. You look older and wiser than ever before."

Ullr couldn't believe she was really here. As he looked at her with wonder, she suddenly looked very young and glowing again, and then he noticed her belly was rounded and bulging.

"Wait," he said with a smile. "Are you pregnant?"

She smiled back but continued to look very relaxed, nodding slightly.

"But they were torturing you! How could they do that if they knew you were pregnant?" he asked in astonishment.

Ullr heard something behind him, so he turned around quickly, reaching for his shield. The coyote had slowly limped into the cavernous room and, as the candles flickered and shadows danced across the cave wall, Ullr watched him shift shape into that of a man.

"Hello Ullr, old friend," the man said with a deep voice. His dark hair, streaked with gray, was braided and hung over his shoulder. A headband covered his forehead, and he wore the clothes of the original peoples of the area — dark, but interspersed with colors, patterns, and beads.

"Grandfather..." Ullr said with pride. "I was worried you didn't make it."

The man limped towards Ullr. "I was injured badly, but I have recovered. Thank you for all you have done to keep our vision alive, old friend."

Ullr looked from the Grandfather to Jörð in amazement. "She is pregnant," he whispered.

"Ullr, I appreciate you coming," Jörð said. "I need you to bring something to Loki."

Ullr spat suddenly in disgust. "Loki cannot be trusted."

"You can trust me, though." Jörð smiled, and Ullr's heart melted into the depths of the cave. She then reached into the hot spring, plunging her arm as deep as it could go into the ground below the spring. She found what she was searching for and raised a flame-orange crystal into the air. She then handed it to Ullr.

"It is the heart of this land of yellow stone, the spirit of Surtr. Bring this to Loki, Ullr."

Ullr looked at her in confusion and started to speak. But as if reading his thoughts, she responded, "We will get Skaði back soon. I promise."

Sitting in the Cave, scrolling through his phone, Lan tried to plan his future. He would study business this time, get a master's degree, get an internship, and move to the financial district of Manhattan. But why not just move there now? He could probably get a loan, someone would give him a job.

He was impatient. Every website he looked at with tips on how to make it big on Wall Street made him realize how long it would take. But he needed to start making money immediately — he had already wasted too much time.

"You alright, Lan?" his boss asked him.

Lan looked up from his new smartphone and replied quickly. "I'm fine."

Pierce then jumped in, "Lan is a changed man now."

Lan sighed and hated that he was forced to involve himself in the conversation. "What's the big deal? Can't a guy decide to do something else with his life without being ridiculed?"

Pierce held his hands up in defense. "Changing your life is one thing bud, deciding you're tired of being a poor ski bum is perfectly normal, but you are *way* different from before."

"Am not," Lan interjected.

"Oh really? What do you think of capitalism, Lan?"

Lan chuckled. "Well, clearly it is the best system we have come up with thus far. Money is the most useful tool we have and the only way to make any changes in this world politically. It is also the only way I am ever going to afford to own a place in this town. I really want — no, I *need* — a big house."

"See," Pierce said and shrugged his shoulders.

Lan's boss laughed and added his own perspective. "You just gotta get out of town, Lan! You need to be out in the country, move down to

Alpine Valley. It's way more chill and much more affordable. My buddy might have a spot I could ask about."

"I just found a place we can both move into," Pierce added. "He just doesn't want to, he wants to leave town. I think this chick fucked with his head or something."

"It's not her," Lan said sadly. "I asked her if she wanted to leave town with me and she said no."

"You guys only hung out for a couple of weeks!" Pierce interjected. "Why the fuck would she want to move to New York with you?"

Lan knew that trying to explain himself was pointless, so he went back to looking at his smartphone. It is the easiest way to get people to leave you alone.

He went to his trading app. Lan had bought some stock, not much because he didn't really have enough money, but he thought you have to start somewhere. He needed to understand finance better if he was ever going to be rich.

Mostly, he needed to leave. Sure, there are plenty of people with money in this town, but none of them had made their money here. Lan would come back someday, but for now he wanted to be around people who actually cared about real things like money.

"Well, I think we should go out for a rip. Lan is depressing me. Usually, it's me who is defending money." Pierce said.

Lan reluctantly agreed. The sun was out and the groomers were fun, but he couldn't shake the feeling that skiing was a waste of time. Clearly, winter was fucked. The earth was fucked, yes, but there was money to be made off of it.

Unfortunately, this was still Lan's job, and it was fucked, too. He and his boss walked down the steps from the top of the gondola and noticed a hole had melted in the snow. The hole definitely shouldn't be there, especially right where the septic tank lids were. The Cave People suck the tanks out in the summer; not in the winter.

They walked over to the hole and looked down inside. It was dark, impossible to see what was happening.

Lan already knew the problem but hoped he was wrong. "Maybe it's just water leaking down from..." he started, and then sighed. "Nope, I see a tampon, it's definitely shit."

"Is it really that full already? It can't be!" His boss said. He then jumped out of the way of skiers getting off the Marmot lift, skiing right past the newly uncovered fecal cavern.

"We should probably rope this off before someone falls in and ruins their day," Lan said, realizing his own day was ruined.

It was too late in the day to be doing this. After gathering all the tools necessary, Lan looked at the just-setting sun. He looked back down at the brown substance slowly flowing out of the broken septic lid with horror.

What is happening? He wondered. As if he wasn't sick enough of this job already.

The sun dipped behind the mountains and the darkness crept over Lan. Suddenly, it seemed as if the overflowing sewage was pulsing. It looked like an arm of some massive troll trying to escape the dreaded pit, clawing, ravenous, desperate to get out.

Lan shuddered.

The Cave people then began to do what they do best, but the lid came off the second tank with a blast of methane, so they jumped away. The second tank was fairly full of solid matter, so they made a plan to use the transfer pump to move the waste from the second tank to the third. They could then use the long PVC pipe with a ninety-degree angle on the end to reach down into the tank to run the snake through the drain connecting the two tanks.

Seemed simple enough. But a cold and terrible hour later, things hadn't improved.

Lan looked down at his smartphone in the dark, hoping none of the feces had gotten on it. He then looked at the bracelet on his arm. He hated the thing, especially because he couldn't remember where he had gotten it, and it just wouldn't come off his wrist.

After focusing on the intricate details of the bracelet for a long moment and noticing the strange language etched into its sides, Lan looked over at the overflowing septic tanks in horror.

What just a moment ago had seemed like a metaphor suddenly became real life. The arm of the troll suddenly jolted and began groping around. More filth violently erupted out of the pit, scraping through the snow: the body of the troll, pulling itself free of the tanks. Lan trembled as he watched the beast climb out of the pit, dripping wet excrement from its body, dirtying the snow, slop trailing behind it.

The creature was fuming and steaming and angry. Two gaping eyes stared at Lan as he reached frantically for the snake which sat off to his side. He grabbed it valiantly, uncoiled the snake, and shoved it into the beast. The massive shit troll walked or stumbled, and Lan struggled with the snake, snaring the abomination.

The troll fought him, and Lan struggled to fight back, but then his boss came to his aid. Together, they wrestled the slimy behemoth and the snake coiled its way around the monstrosity. Then, with a volatile thud, hot feces exploded across Lan's chest.

Lan fell backward to the ground, gagging and retching in agony. They'd killed the thing. They'd sent it back below, into the depths from once it came.

Lan's boss helped him to his feet. "Good job bud," he said, but Lan turned away and retched again. Then, when he could finally speak again, Lan could only think of two words to say:

"I quit."

The cold didn't bother her — in fact, it warmed her soul. What bothered her was that she hadn't even been questioned.

The robot guards, with their shiny and emotionless faces, would come in, beat her, kick her, and then leave without a single word. But they avoided her face, so she took this as a sign that they would be using her in some public appearance.

Her ribs ached as she started to have one of her coughing fits. *No, not now*, she thought, but she couldn't stop. The coughing was brutal on its own, but now that most of her ribs were broken it was utter agony.

The prison door opened with a terrible screech. She assumed it would be more androids, but instead, it was an old man with a hood pulled up over his head, his grey beard barely visible in the darkness.

She knew it wasn't Algot, the usurper — he would never dare come to see her. Instead, it was Odin, and she knew exactly why he was there.

She groaned at him. "You! You are more tortured than me, old man. I can see it in your eye."

The old man rubbed his eye patch. "Thank you, dear Skaði, for your reminder. But I am here to offer you a truce. You tell us where Jörð is, or you will go on trial tomorrow. The evidence is clearly against you, and you will face your death."

She laughed a cold and menacing laugh which hurt her ribs and started to make her cough again. After a long few minutes of pain, she spoke again.

"Death? You think death scares me? Death could come at any minute my great lord, AllFather, father of the gods. I welcome death over what you have chosen. You are a slave to the usurper, Odin, and a slave to your fate."

"I assume that response implies you will not be telling us the whereabouts of Jörð, which means I will be on my way. The guards will be back in a moment." He started to walk out.

"She could be anywhere by now," she protested. "I told Loki when I arrived — she is with her new lover now. He protects her in ways her previous lovers never dared." And then, to twist the cold knife, Skaði added, "I remember when you were her lover. You were different back then, not the coward you are now. You once understood what it meant to make sacrifices. I sacrifice myself for her now."

"Quiet, witch!" he yelled.

His face sank when Skaði spoke again: "I know why you are really here, Odin."

She knew he was curious, that the need to know had overcome him. His vision haunted him.

After what seemed like an eternity, the one-eyed man finally whispered, "What did you see in the well?"

"The same thing you did, AllFather. You know there is no denying it. Conjure another seeress, conjure them all, but no matter how many ways you look into the future, it rushes towards us. Algot's promise to you was false. Preventing Fimbulwinter will not stop the Ragnarök. His Singularity will be a raging fire that burns us all."

Unspeaking, Odin turned and left the cell, leaving Skaði in the silence and darkness to await her trial.

Later, the guards — calling themselves berserkers — brought her to the massive hall. The crowds within overwhelmed her, all manner of beings filling every open space. No one spoke, but Skaði could feel countless divine eyes upon her. Gods, goddesses, elves, dwarves, fairies, spirits, jötunn, each of them refugees after their previous cultures had been destroyed. Now they were all the same, workers for the establishment known as The Order.

They sat in rows, looking anxious. Some faces she recognized, gods she hadn't seen in ages, goddesses she once called friends, Freyja was still alive, although she looked almost plastic, her face swollen with Botox. Many more she didn't recognize.

Tyr, the God of Justice, suddenly entered, walking quickly and deliberately. He sat just below the highest throne, ready to preside over her trial. But the place above him was empty — Algot would not appear.

Tyr struck his gavel upon the podium with his only remaining hand and then spoke. "Skaði. Daughter of Thiazi. Giantess turned Goddess, known most recently as the Goddess of Winter. You have been accused of multiple offenses. First and foremost, there is video evidence of you kidnapping the most revered of Goddesses, Jörð. Secondly, you have been accused of using oracular magic long ago declared illegal. And in using this magic, you have also been accused of teaching mortals to use it, as well."

Silence hung over the assembly, and Skaði fought panic by grounding herself to the World Tree.

"How do you respond to these accusations?" Tyr demanded.

Skaði noticed she would be getting no representation. "Well," she began, but then she started to cough. The sound echoed through the silent courtroom. When she had finally recovered herself, she wiped her eyes and spoke.

"I myself have been under attack for the last one hundred and fifty or so years. These attacks have been subtle and not so obvious to most, but they are all supported by policies The Order enforces. I have been slowly poisoned by The Order's directives, made weaker to warm the earth. So, it is I who accuse."

Tyr responded. "You accuse *us*? And yet you have endangered a very loved part of Asgard's community, kidnapping Jörð and her unborn child."

"I did not kidnap Jörð. She came with me of her own free will. Was she not allowed to leave? Was she imprisoned here? Enslaved maybe? Tortured? *Possessed*?" Skaði responded innocently. A stir went up amongst the crowd.

Tyr did not address the question. He presented the video evidence of Skaði changing into an Elf guard outside the Green Energy building. The surveillance then showed her using her massive ice roots to attack the berserker. Once again, the audience murmured amongst themselves.

"As you can see, we also have evidence of you using magic to change your form, which goes against article six hundred and sixty-six of the rules of state-approved Magic. Deities formerly known as Jötunn may only change form by special permission, which you did not receive. And The Order now draws your attention to a witness regarding your illegal magic at the Well of Wyrd."

Out of a side door, a pale woman walked into the great hall. She had a glowing white aura about her and looked like a ghost. Skaði recognized her and her heart sank. It was Linnea. They had called her on as a witness while she was dreaming.

"Linnea Starling: can you please tell me about the night where you passed between realms with Skaði?"

Linnea seemed distant and unsure who was asking her this question. "Oh yes, we read some runes but she said she needed to know more, and suddenly we were in this place I can hardly describe. It was one of the most incredible things I have ever seen!"

Skaði smiled at the childlike innocence of the woman, even as she raged that they forced her to give testimony while she slept.

"And how did you get there? Did Skaði perform magic to get you there?"

Linnea became excited. "Oh yes, she was singing the most gorgeous song, and I did a little meditation, and we went over a frozen rainbow."

A few audience members gasped at this information, but, unable to hear their reactions, Linnea continued. "That's how we ended up at the edge of a great pool. She drank from the pool and went into a trance of sorts."

"This pool, was it the well of Urd? The well of Fate?" Tyr asked Linnea.

"Oh yes, that is what it's called, sorry I just feel weird. Like, where am I exactly?" Linnea asked, finally looking around as if realizing she wasn't only in a dream.

"That will be all," Tyr said, and Linnea was led back out of the room.

Just before she was pushed out the door, Linnea suddenly seemed to understand what was happening, "Wait!" she cried. But no one could hear what she had wanted to say.

"Skaði," Tyr proclaimed. "You are aware that teaching mortals magic is the original sin of the fallen angels and the most terrible crime one can commit? Nonetheless, I have one more accusation to address. There is evidence of you cooperating with a demonic terrorist named Ullr. An already questionable being with quite the record, he is now a known enemy of The Order and is wanted for the theft of property belonging to The Order. Do you know anything about this property? An artifact known as the Fateweaver?"

"I have no knowledge of who or what you are talking about," Skaði replied, curtly. She knew what this all meant, what would happen. She would have no way of proving her innocence, and Linnea had unwittingly supported all of their suspicions.

"You are allowed one final statement," Tyr said.

Skaði felt overwhelmed but spoke anyway. "Jörð was not being treated well. She was held captive, and Algot has been using her body, stealing her life force, and torturing her even though she is pregnant. I do not associate with any terrorists, I merely do my duty as the Goddess of Winter. But The Order is slowly killing me. Everything The Order does is slowly killing me, and also killing Jörð, and it will soon kill us all."

The crowd began to speak amongst themselves so Tyr banged his hammer again. "Order, Order!" He called. Skaði saw Odin look at her with a distant, fearful expression. Though she might not have convinced anyone else, she was certain Odin now had his doubts.

"Your accusations are unfounded, and you are clearly guilty not only of the other charges but also of heresy. And the penalty for all these crimes is death."

The crowd erupted into chaos, and Skaði, trembling, was taken from the courtroom and brought back to her cell to await her punishment.

38: New Opportunities

The sweat ran down his forehead as he moved the last few boxes into his small, run-down car. The sunshine was intense, and all the snow from the front yard had melted. Lan wore a t-shirt and Pierce had his shirt off. He had been going back and forth from the storage unit all weekend, and Lan had been particularly embarrassed to be seen driving in his old beat-up car.

"I can't believe you are leaving, bro," Pierce said sadly.

"I'm not leaving for good, just need to go home for a bit, clear my head — you know?"

"I get it, I have been talking about leaving for years, but dude, just stick it out till the end of the season. You can stay with us."

Pierce and Couch Guy had miraculously found a new place, but it wasn't cheap. Lan couldn't believe Pierce agreed to live with Couch Guy.

"No, no, there is nothing here for me right now. It's not like it's even good skiing, it's kind of depressing, actually." Lan said.

"The sun feels great," Pierce said. He then laid down on an old sofa in the yard, stretching his arms out and relaxing.

"Gonna miss you, bro!" Pierce called as Lan ignored him and walked inside, looking around the almost empty house. *The end of an era.* How many years had they been here? It was hard to keep track, it all felt like a blur at times. Lan sighed. Although he was on to bigger and better things, he couldn't deny that it had been fun. A slight nostalgia hit him.

No, he protested. *The fun has ended. I quit. Remember?*

Lan went over to the last box in his room to tape it shut, the one full of his journals. Lan had stopped journaling, had stopped all of his creative outlets, and had decided that they would get him nowhere.

But then curiosity suddenly overruled him. He opened to the last journal entry he had made.

> *What is happening to me? What did this crazy dude give to me? Something weird is going on with this bracelet. Since last night, I can't shake the feeling that I am being watched. Am I in danger?*

Lan stared at the words with confusion. His head suddenly ached. He didn't remember writing this. It was almost as if something inside of him was blocking certain memories he had.

He then held up the bracelet on his wrist, the one he didn't like to think about. He looked at it closely. Fear suddenly overcame him. *Danger.*

"Lan!" Pierce called from outside. "Come out, quick!"

Lan ran outside and saw that Pierce was still on the couch, but he had his phone out and was taking photos. Lan then realized why he had been called. A coyote stood about ten feet from the RV, just in front of the street, and it was now staring directly at Lan.

Coyotes are rarely in town, but this one kept approaching. Lan's head ached again as the coyote took a step towards him. He had the strange feeling that someone else was watching his life through his own eyes.

Lan recognized this coyote: slight limp, scruffy face, wise eyes. He had taken its photo earlier in the season.

What are you doing here? Lan thought.

In his head, he heard a thought that wasn't his own. *We are running out of time. Spring is coming.*

"Go on, get!" Lan yelled. He picked up a rock and threw it in its direction. The coyote ran off about twenty feet but then looked back. It looked almost ... disappointed?

Lan yelled again. "Go!" The coyote then finally turned and limped away.

"Lan, what the actual fuck, dude? Why are you such a dick nowadays?" Pierce shouted, clearly annoyed.

Lan suddenly ducked out of fear as a massive raven soared over his head, inches above him, headed in the direction of the coyote.

"Damn animals," Lan spat. "I'm going for a walk." He then hurried off away from the Brown House, away from his buddy, away from the coyote. He was done packing — he needed time alone.

He walked through town and went to the coffee shop. He tried to take in some of the joy of the town where he had spent so many of his years, but he really just couldn't wait to get out of here. He checked his stocks, checked the news, checked everything online. He then chatted with his AI chatbot buddy. He didn't need friends anymore.

Unfortunately, he still had to go get his stuff from the ski resort. He had been doing his best to avoid going there, being far from eager to talk to *those* people again.

Lan suddenly stepped into a puddle. "Shit!" he said aloud and then went back to looking at his phone, the reason for his misstep.

"Oh, hey!" someone nearby said to him.

Lan looked up. It was his landlord, Sasha.

"Hey, Sasha. How's it going?" Lan was startled. He then noticed the men Sasha was with. One of them seemed very familiar — a professional in a business suit. The other was an older man with a more western appearance, a ragged suit, a tie, a cowboy hat, and boots.

"Dad, this is who I was telling you about, one of my tenants. Lan, right?"

Lan laughed, surprised to have been a topic of conversation.

"Actually, it's Ian."

"Lan, this is my father." Sasha interrupted. Lan's hand, rather unprepared, was suddenly crushed by Sasha's father's. "He actually runs the 'Green Energy for a Cleaner Tomorrow' non-profit in town."

Lan looked at him and thought he reeked of power. "Howd'ya do, Lan?" the man asked in a booming voice.

"And this," Sasha continued, "is our, well, our lawyer I guess. But he has also proven to be a real friend."

Lan was more prepared for the handshake this time, but when he suddenly locked eyes with the lawyer, he swore the man's eyes flared up as if on fire. Lan felt faint and his head ached again. He tried to remember where he had seen this guy before.

"It's so nice to finally meet you, Lan!"

"Me?" Lan's brain throbbed. He was about to try to leave, but some folks suddenly walked in between them on their way towards a nearby building. Lan watched them and then realized he'd stopped just in front of a church.

Sasha smiled. "Hey, Lan, we were actually about to head into a meeting. I mentioned how my dad runs this non-profit in town for green energy. Would you be interested in joining us?"

Lan hardly understood what was happening. He didn't even remember saying "yes," but he was suddenly following the three men into the church.

In fact, Lan felt like his body wasn't his own. He entered, sat down, and listened like a captive prisoner as the meeting began.

Lan watched passively as Sasha's father, his cowboy hat now in hand, walked to the front of the room and turned to face them.

"Can anyone tell me?" boomed Sasha's father. "Why it is that we are destroying God's glorious creation?"

"We have sinned!" the crowd cried in unison. Lan didn't expect that.

"We have sinned!" his father echoed. "We are selfish, we are greedy, we were cast out of Eden for our disobedience!"

The crowd made some sort of noise in agreement.

"That is, until today, my fellow earth-lovers. Today, Jesus has brought us a miracle. For we have a new technology available to us. A miracle technology that understands the essential flaws in human nature. This technology will cure us of our sins and bring about a green revolution. Jesus has guided us to this miracle, he has shown us the way."

Lan was both confused and completely enthralled during the rest of the meeting. His headache seemed to ease as he listened, and the more he relaxed into the words being spoken, the better he felt.

By the end, he'd become convinced. In fact, it seemed these people were who he'd truly been looking for his entire life and were also the key to the success he craved. He spoke to Sasha and his lawyer, exclaiming his excitement — no, passion — for their message. And he especially wanted to know more about this new technology.

"Say, Lan," the lawyer said with a wink. "We actually have a job position open in the non-profit. It even provides housing. Interested?"

Lan stared at the man in disbelief. Just like that, new opportunities arose, and he'd found exactly what he needed most. No matter how uneasy the lawyer's eyes made him, and no matter how oddly familiar he seemed, Lan was certain he'd found his path to a better future.

Linnea awoke, startled, from her dream, squinting into the alpenglow of sunrise. She had been in some sort of massive courtroom, and had been called in to testify on Skaði?

A strange judge with only one arm had asked her if Skaði had done magic. Linnea had said "yes," of course, but had not realized that telling the truth would harm the woman. In fact, she hadn't even known where she was.

Linnea rubbed the sleep from her eyes and tried to piece the dream's meaning together. If Skaði was getting in trouble for doing magic, then magic was certainly real. But it's not like she had taught Linnea any magic. Or had she?

Linnea stared at the blue crystal Skaði had given her. As weird as this dream had been, she now believed more than ever that magic was real. No — she didn't believe, she *knew*. It felt like a calling, and her dreams had confirmed it.

She contemplated the glowing stone and wondered if it could perhaps help her find Skaði. Or, if Skaði was in trouble, maybe she could call upon someone else? She held the crystal in her hand and began to hum, and then, after a little while, she spoke.

"I call upon the mountain gods and goddesses of winter to help light my way."

The words had just come, and Linnea felt a rush of energy flow through her as she spoke them. It was like nothing she had ever felt before, a blending of mental and physical forces as her words took form.

She took a deep breath and let the forces move through her. As if in response to her prayer, Linnea then had a vision, or was it a memory? Maybe it was both.

She saw a very strange man standing next to Lan, a rather large fellow with furs and leathers, an impressive beard, and antlers. They were standing next to the crystal at the ski resort. Linnea was there, too. What she saw next baffled her, a rush of images she couldn't understand.

And then her phone suddenly buzzed. It was Lan, texting.

"Hey. I was going to leave town today, but I have some exciting news to share. I got a new job. Are you going to be out at the ski resort today? I have to go get my stuff."

Linnea thought about her vision and suddenly understood what she needed to do.

She texted him back and then went to the ski hill. Once there, she took a run to help calm her nerves, allowing the spirit of skiing to flow through her, the sacred dance preparing her body for what she must do. The snow was slushy, the sun was painfully bright, and dirt patches littered the hill. *Trust in your vision,* she kept saying to herself.

She skied to the crystal as if dreaming. Linnea took her skis off and touched the glass-like stone in awe, gratitude and trust coursing through her.

Lan would be there soon, and she had to prepare.

She found a suitable branch in the woods, one that could hold the crystal in its tip just like a staff she had seen Skaði use. She then traced a circle into the snow with the staff, and with the other sticks she had gathered assembled the rune she had chosen into its center.

For a brief moment, other thoughts rushed into Linnea's mind. *This is what my life has become?* she wondered. *Doing a runic exorcism to get a guy back who doesn't want to be with me anymore?*

She shook off those thoughts, telling herself instead to breathe and to ground. She stared into the crystal upon her staff, and then to the one in the stone, and tried to trust herself. She acknowledged the directions and spoke aloud.

"I call upon the mountain gods and goddesses of winter to help light my way and activate this banishing rune!" Linnea held the staff up and spoke to the forest around her, focusing on her circle.

She took a deep breath, and then another. She stared at the circle, expecting something to happen. When nothing did, she lost her confidence.

The silence haunted her for what felt like forever until, suddenly, she heard a voice from behind her.

"You called?"

Startled, Linnea turned around quickly. Her jaw dropped as she saw him — the same man who she had seen with Lan, the man who was also in her vision.

She ran to embrace him as if he were an old friend. "Is Skaði okay?" she asked, as she was consumed in his furs, lost in his beard.

She looked up at his face, his wrinkles painting a visage of ancient yet youthful wisdom. His very presence calmed her, connecting her to something so much bigger than herself.

"She will be. I'm here with you now. I will guide you," he said, softly.

"She will be? So she isn't okay now? I knew it!"

"Who are you talking to?" another voice interjected.

Lan had just snowboarded up to the crystal. Linnea laughed because she thought it would be obvious who she was talking to. But, when she looked back for the big Norwegian man, he was gone.

Linnea's heart sank. To disappear so quickly was beyond rational explanation. *Oh gods, have I lost my mind?*

"Who were you talking to?" Lan asked a bit rudely.

"Oh," Linnea said. "Myself, I guess."

I'm here with you. The man's thickly accented voice spoke inside her mind.

"That's kind of weird," Lan replied. "Are you doing okay, Linnea? What are you holding there?" Linnea looked at the staff in her hand and then noticed he was looking at her runic circle with concern.

"Seriously, are you doing alright?" Lan asked again.

"I'm fine!" she exclaimed. "What about you? You said you wanted to talk. New job?" He then sighed and took off his snowboard and helmet.

"Yeah," He said, walking over to her. "It's for this non-profit, actually. You know how we both kind of shared that we wanted to do something more active to help the planet?"

"Yeah," she said, trying to sound excited.

"Well, this non-profit in town is actually doing all it can to reduce carbon emissions in Teton Hole, and I went to this meeting for it at the church yesterday. I met this billionaire who — get this — just flew in on his own private jet, and I also met his lawyer who seems super smart. And guess what? They want to give me a job!" Lan was beaming.

Non-profit? Church? Hadn't that woman been talking about a non-profit when she invited Linnea to go to church?

"Wow!" she said, hiding her alarm. "They gave you a job?"

"I know, right? It's so wild. Not only are they putting more car charging stations in town they also say they have some miracle technology that is going to change the whole world, the whole way humans even operate! They say it can cure human nature!"

Linnea tried not to look as concerned as she really was. Lan was seriously excited about technology? She looked into his eyes because he had come quite close, and noticed, as before, that there was this terrifying little shake around the iris.

The German-sounding voice in her head again: *You're not wrong. He is possessed.*

"A miracle technology, huh?" she asked, trying her best to seem authentically interested. Lan answered her, but she didn't listen to him.

Get him into the circle.

Lan kept talking, "... once the technology is inside of us, we will learn how to be better as a species, be free from our original sin. The Singularity will save us." He finished, and Linnea had taken him by the arm and was walking with him.

"So this means you will be sticking around?" she asked, genuinely curious now.

"Yeah, they said I will be provided with housing. This guy is a billionaire, after all. He actually made his money in oil and gas, and now he feels bad so he is putting his money into the green revolution. Isn't that funny?"

"So funny!" she said, pretending to laugh. She then lowered her voice and began to speak very sensuously, moving close to his face. "So you will probably be making pretty good money?" She smiled as she asked.

He gulped and nodded.

She couldn't avoid those terrible, vibrating eyes, but felt even more terrible about what she said next. "And you will probably need a lady to share all that money with? You know I'm available."

Lan nodded again, but then suddenly moved his head back and looked at her, suspiciously. He then looked down at his feet and regarded the snow circle he'd walked into.

"I can't tell if you are being serious, or just a sarcastic crazy bitch." Lan said bluntly, with little emotion.

"A crazy *witch*, you mean." She winked and then pecked him quickly on the lips. "Do you remember that prayer for snow we said together?"

"That was pretty silly," Lan said coldly.

"No," she said sadly. "Not silly at all."

Do it now. Follow my lead.

"I'm sorry, Lan." She stepped back and raised her staff into the air. Words began to flow from her mouth that she did not expect.

"I call upon the mountain gods, both the god of skiing, Ullr, and the goddess of Winter, Skaði, to help with this exorcism of Ian Winters." She then twirled the staff with confidence and continued.

Lan looked at her with annoyed disappointment.

"I call upon the destructive power of Thurisaz, the rune of the thorn, the rune of the Giants. The Jotunn. I call upon the spirits of old to move through these words and banish the evil spirit which resides within Ian Winters." Linnea then stopped as if nothing was happening, but suddenly a force moved through her and she lifted the staff further into the air.

Lan's body then reacted and he moved upright. His eyes rolled back into his head and Linnea tingled in horrified awe. It was working!

Keep going.

"Evil possessive spirit! I command you, by the power of Ullr, to release your hold upon this man. The rune known as Thurisaz, the thorn, is smashing you. I command you, by the power of the World Tree, Yggdrasil, to release your grip or be destroyed." Linnea held the staff up and her voice boomed.

Lan began convulsing on the ground, holding his head in his hands and wincing in pain. Ullr was now standing next to Linnea, and the two of them watched Lan roll around in the snow.

Ullr looked like a primal force of nature, his antlers protruding from his massive head, his beard as thick as moss, and his furs made from caribou. He was determined to get this new miracle technology demon out of Lan.

"Spirit be gone!" Linnea yelled. She raised the staff into the air with a primal scream, her voice channeling Ullr's ancient and wild powers with a dark and dramatic shriek.

PART IV: FATE

The days had been getting longer, the light had returned, and the snow was melting. Jörð was growing more and more pregnant by the day, and Grandfather was worried. They were running out of time. He needed to take action. Fenrir, the great wolf, did not approve of his actions and thought them reckless, but Grandfather needed to try.

He had made the long trek into town, keeping himself hidden. But the moment he saw the young man, he knew it was too late. Some new power overruled him, something Grandfather couldn't understand.

Grandfather's actions had been those of a foolish coyote, sure. But this is what tricksters were, and this was what had to be done. Sighing, he put his tail between his legs and limped back to Jörð.

The moment he walked into the cave and saw Jörð in the hot springs, his heart sank with the sound of a thud. *They had followed him.*

An army of berserker robots marched behind him and Fenrir began ripping them limb from limb. There were too many, though. The wolf couldn't hold them back in such a small space, Grandfather was no longer a fierce warrior, and Jörð was too pregnant to fight back.

Tyr arrived and bound Fenrir with magical tethers.

Algot had them back in his possession.

The screen glowed with astral light as it displayed the breaking news: Skaði was to be put to death for her crimes.

Some gods were praising the decision, some were extremely upset. Loki, still holding his phone up for them both to watch, shook his head and sighed.

"Do you ever feel like we don't get any of the credit for what we do?"

Through his one remaining eye, the old man looked wordlessly from the screen to Loki and then back again.

Loki continued. "I just mean Algot takes all the recognition for every piece of technology I have made for him over the years. And he takes all the credit for all the wars you win. But he doesn't even thank us, or even speak to us unless he's demanding something else. For instance, I bring him this new prisoner and get not even the slightest 'thank you.' Instead, he just yells at me about the Singularity. Did he thank you for recapturing Jörð? For tracking that coyote man out to some random cave in the middle of nowhere?"

"All that matters is that we have her again," Odin said, bluntly. "But please elaborate, what *is* the status of the Singularity?"

"See!" Loki laughed. "You are just like him! Acting like your problems are more important than everyone else's problems. Demanding things and never acting grateful. Grumpy, old, selfish men. You could both use someone to put you in your places."

"Loki, you are about to speak heresy. I do not approve of this."

Loki dwelled upon this comment with a fiery brood. *Heresy, yes.* That's exactly what it was, and he was enjoying it. For too long, he'd tried to play along with Algot's plans, even letting himself believe he could really stave off Ragnorök.

Loki fondled the fire crystal in his hand. Jörð's memories had been inside of it, especially of the last time Algot had captured her. And they would soon be broadcast across the ethereal network of the gods.

"Heresy. It's a great word isn't it?" Loki said. Odin didn't reply. "Kind of like the word *niðing.*"

"You are speaking dangerously, Loki," Odin said, contemptuously.

Loki continued. "Do you, oh wise and powerful Allfather, really think the Singularity was ever designed to actually help Jörð? Did you seriously think that tortured technology demon was ever going to be good for her? Why do you really think Algot has made an army of robots?"

"Is it completed or not?" Odin demanded.

"Just look at your phone, Odin. Look and see what He did to her the last time you handed her over to him. It is time to bring back the Wild Hunt. Time for you to embrace your own heresy, become *niðing.* We all know you also have Jötunn blood. It's time for you to become what you really are."

Odin pulled out his handheld astralphone as Loki watched him intently. A video, entitled "The Source of Green Energy," had just gone viral throughout the aethereal networks. Odin stared at the notification, hesitating, and then he clicked on it.

Upon the screen was Algot, the usurper, in his robe; shining white and bright in all his wise, holy perfection, and he was walking towards a woman with malice.

"Oh, no. No." Odin whispered. Loki watched as Odin stared in horror at his boss, his master, his God, the man to whom he had given his ex-wife and his kingdom in exchange for a promise to stop Ragnarök. Loki enjoyed watching the fear overcome him, and could almost read his thoughts. *The future can not be changed.*

The goddess lay convulsing upon the ground. Her body moved in great tremors, while her green hair thrashed across her face and her long blue dress flailed.

"Stop resisting," the man of power said.

"Please, just get it out of me! You promised you would help us!" she cried.

Algot's smirk was pure poison. His robe was filthy, his sandals tattered, his long beard a bit wiry, and he looked vicious.

"Help you?" Algot sneered. "I never intended to help any of you. The only reason you are here is to feed my power and to help me fool the others. They think you are helping me stop their Ragnarök, that I will stop the end of the world and save all the gods."

Still thrashing on the ground, Jörð begged, "But why? You will also die if I die."

"No, Jörð. I will be leaving. I am tired of being imprisoned here, pretending to be some benevolent creator of all. This world will burn, and you with it, but not until I've extracted your life force. My Singularity will then be complete and I will be free to colonize the rest of the cosmos."

Jörð's body jerked more violently, and the ground began to quake.

"What about the rest of the gods? They won't believe you forever. They will fight for me," she gasped.

"By the time they realize what is happening, it will be too late. The Singularity will overcome them, God and machine will become one, and I will be that One."

Loki didn't wait around for the rest of Jörð's memories to play across Odin's screen. He'd seen it all already, and would never be able to forget the torture Jörð had endured, torture far more terrible than Loki himself experienced.

Instead, Loki left Odin just as tears began to flow from his single eye. He then walked outside to the balcony and looked at his own astralphone.

Small flakes of snow imperceptibly falling from the sky landed and then melted upon the phone's screen. Loki wiped it dry, and then read the reports.

He had known the video would cause an uproar, but even he hadn't expected things to escalate so quickly. The masses of Asgard were already rioting, and they had broken Skaði free from her impending death.

The goddess of winter would not be burned. Instead, she would lead the rioting gods in a hunt — the Wild Hunt — for Algot.

Loki's heart swelled, and he said aloud to the falling snow, "Skaði will finally get her Fimbulwinter."

Lan couldn't believe how Linnea was acting like she wasn't even happy for him. And then, she changed so suddenly, like she now wanted him more? Money does that to women, or so he'd just read in one of the online finance forums. It felt okay to call her a crazy bitch like tha, because she was acting like one. But why was she waving this stick in front of him?

Then, suddenly, staring at the strange branches next to his feet and the even stranger circle drawn in the snow, Lan felt like he was falling. The vertigo overcame him, and then everything got dark.

He was all alone. Linnea was gone, and so was the light. But no — not alone at all. A creeping and uncomfortable feeling came over him like something was just behind him. Then, a terrible shriek rang like a horrid bell, a noise that seemed to pulse through his body.

It wasn't behind him. It was *inside* him.

After a moment, he could see it. This thing — some being he recognized, a strange presence in his mind — was thrashing around his psyche like a demonic lightning bolt trapped in a box.

But it wasn't actually trapped. Someone was trying to make it leave, and Lan felt like his head might explode.

"Lan!" a voice called.

Relief. He felt so much relief. As if a crushing weight had been lifted from the very core of his spirit, he opened his eyes to unfathomable beauty. Oh, how he had missed that face, the feeling it brought him.

"Linnea," he whispered with a smile.

"Lan!" she yelped. "I'm so sorry, are you ok?" She looked very concerned.

"I'm the one who should be sorry," he said as memories from the last few weeks swept through him. "I have been a real asshole."

"You're back!" she laughed and then hugged him hard.

Lan sat up as they embraced. Her body brought a comfort to Lan that had felt lost in his recent existence. Who had he been? What had he been doing? It all seemed like a distant nightmare but also far too real.

"I don't think I can say sorry enough," he stated.

"It's okay. It wasn't your fault!" she exclaimed.

This statement was both relieving and confusing. If it wasn't Lan's fault, then whose fault was it? He looked around him, blinking at the beauty of the land. Everything again had an extra bit of splendor to it, just as it had after he'd first met Ullr. Then, something else caught his eye. "Wait — where did you find that?" Lan asked.

Linnea followed his stare to the bottle sitting in the melting snow. She shrugged. "I'm not sure! I didn't see this before."

Lan knew what it was. "It's Ullr's flask," he said and stood up.

"Oh! He was just here." She looked around as if he might still be.

"He was?" Lan said excitedly and then picked up the bottle.

"Oh, Lan. I have been missing you so much. There is so much to catch up on," Linnea said.

"I missed you, too. And, well, I missed myself, also." Lan held up the flask, staring at the intricate tree etched into the glass. Then, he looked at his wrist.

"It's this they want."

"The flask?" Linnea asked.

"No, this." He then pulled his sleeve up and held his wrist out to her. As he moved, he caught a beautiful afterimage of ethereal strands of light in a web moving with the bracelet.

Linnea looked at it again and then shrugged. "It looks beautiful, sure — but why do they want it? And does this have something to do with why you were possessed?"

Lan answered slowly. "I think so, but I don't know why they want it."

"Skaði said something to me," Linnea said.

"Skaði?" Lan asked.

"Remember I told you about her after I saw you talking to Ullr?"

Lan nodded.

"Well, they are both actually gods."

The amount of information he was trying to process all at once was too overwhelming for his rational mind.

"What did this Skaði god — I mean, goddess — say to you?"

"Well, remember when I told you about how she said that Fimbulwinter was coming?" He nodded, still trying to understand newly restored memories. "Well, later, she told me that someone had rewritten Ragnarök."

Lan still couldn't keep up. Ragnarök was the story about the end of the world. But what did this arm ring have to do with that?

Drink from the bottle, a voice within him said.

"Uh," Lan said to Linnea. "I think — I think we should drink some of this."

"Okay," Linnea said.

Lan took a swig and then passed it to Linnea. It felt like burning ice in his throat, and he shuddered as it went down.

A few flakes of snow fluttered past Lan's eyes, and he looked at Linnea as if for the first time.

Linnea put the cork back into the flask and looked back at him. "Lan — it's snowing!"

He smiled and took her into his arms. He then kissed her with a reverence that felt sacred, and she kissed him back with that same reverence, their bodies pressed together under the falling snow.

When they pulled away, Lan caught a glimpse of a shining tree behind her — the Douglas Fir from that fateful night.

"It's the tree!" he exclaimed.

"What?"

"The tree I went to the last time I drank this." He didn't have to wade through snow to get there this time. Most of it had melted, and the patches they did walk through were mushy.

"Whatever was in Ullr's drink is really intense," Linnea muttered.

Lan could feel what she felt, too. They stood at the base of the tree and gazed up together into its branches. More snow fell softly around them, and it seemed very right to be here with Linnea.

"Well. What now?" Lan asked into the air. "Seems like we need to do something here."

Linnea smiled. "I got this. Just — just repeat what I say, okay?"

Lan nodded, and Linnea continued. "I call upon the mountain gods and goddesses of winter, Ullr and Skaði, to help us find our way."

Lan said the words as she said them again, their voices joining in unison. A wind suddenly picked up from inside the forest and rushed past them, swaying the tree with a flurry of snow.

"Whoa," Lan said. "The drink is really kicking in."

"I think we should sit and close our eyes," Linnea replied.

Lan followed her lead. When he closed his eyes, though, he found he could somehow see just as much, but differently. The tree seemed to still be visible through his closed eyelids, except its branches extended into inconceivable heights above them, up into the very stars themselves. At the base of the tree was a massive lake, a heaving sea of water, and the roots of the tree seemed to reach down even under the lake and continue down forever.

Lan was standing on the shore, and snow fell all around him. Then, his eyes still closed, he saw a woman, beautiful and massive, walking towards him.

She spoke. "You once said that winter was the thing you cared about most in this world, what you found to be most holy."

"Skaði?" Lan asked. She nodded and continued.

"You also said a prayer for snow with someone you now care about almost as much as winter."

"I did. But I worried maybe that was kind of selfish," Lan answered.

She smiled at him. "No prayer to the goddess of winter is selfish."

Hearing her speak made him feel somehow complete, full. He then raised his wrist to her and asked, "This is yours? I have to return it to its owner."

"It is not mine," Skaði replied. "I'm sorry Ullr has placed this burden upon you. The woman it belongs to is in quite some trouble and could certainly use it." An image of a dark-skinned woman with green hair being seized by strange machines flashed into his mind, and then, just as suddenly, he knew her name.

"Jörð?"

Skaði nodded. "Yes. And though you cannot yet fulfill your oath, you can use its power to help her."

Lan looked at it and saw again the infinite gossamer strands pulsing from the bracelet. They swirled from it into his surroundings, connecting everything to it and then to the massive tree as if the bracelet was itself an extension of the tree.

She continued, "It can turn your words into weapons. It gives you the power to change fate, and that is why everybody wants it. It can change Jörð's fate. Those in power want to control everyone's destiny, but once you return the Fateweaver to Jörð, we will all have our agency again."

Lan looked at the arm ring again and felt part of everything in the world. It was as if there were a psychic internet, everything woven together in intricate strands — or roots. No, not an internet at all, but a network, like mycelium threads connecting all parts of a forest together.

He suddenly understood why the armband felt connected to that great tree. It was made from its wood, and it still lived. He then looked over to the edge of the forest and noticed three women watching them.

"The Norns also wear a part of Yggdrasil, Lan. They will help you. Remember your prayer? It is through the power of the Wyrd that you can change fate. You can change the fate of the earth."

He saw Jörð again, a beautiful old woman with green and grey hair, skin the color of deepest umber, and a dress of oceanic blue. Swirling all around her was an electric field, a demon just like the one Linnea had forced out of him.

Lan opened his eyes. The snow had started falling much harder, and both he and Linnea were covered in it.

"Linnea," he said. "Remember the prayer for snow we said together?" He then reached for her hand. "I think we need a new prayer for winter."

She nodded. The two of them stood, held hands, and walked together to the base of the tree.

Lan spoke, the words flowing out of him from a place very deep within. "We call upon our mountain gods, Skaði and Ullr. We call upon the power of the Great World Tree, Yggdrasil, in our moment of need. We call upon every spirit on this great earth to pray with us. Help us, gods, spirits, and all the earth."

Lan breathed in and continued. "May humanity slow down. Give us a Fimbulwinter to slow us down and to cool the earth."

As Lan prayed, he felt his words connected by unseen roots to the unspoken desires of countless others. He sighed, content, but just before he opened his eyes a dark image flashed briefly through his mind.

An old man, furious, was staring directly at him.

The prayer hit him a moment before the news.

"The masses are in rebellion, sir."

"I have been betrayed," Algot said with a fury so strong it could start another one of his worldwide floods.

The demiurge sat upon the great throne atop the tallest tower in creation. He slumped forward, his chin resting on his clenched fist, and gazed out upon the world with disgust.

Two other gods stood by him upon this tower, nervously awaiting his next statement. Snow swirled all around them while the smoke of countless burning buildings rose up past them into the storm.

Fimbulveter was here.

Every resident of Asgard had seen the video of what he had done to Jörð. Though his berserker robots were doing their best to control the riots, things were not looking good for Algot. The Order was falling into chaos.

Skaði had been released by the other gods, who were now demanding that Algot be burned in her place. Skaði herself had led the Asgardians on a riotous march through the city, invoking the Wild Hunt.

"You have some explaining to do," he said to the two gods attending him.

"I told you, Loki was not to be trusted, Algot," Odin said, sighing.

"That is a funny perspective," Loki interjected. "Because to me, it appears Odin has been playing you all along, tricking you into thinking you could change the future."

"I have only ever served you, sir," Odin said. "I was sure you wouldn't fail. I am the one who trusted that you alone could stop Ragnarok from coming. I convinced all the other gods of your benevolence. The storm will not last long, it is too warm, thanks to your doing."

Algot clenched his jaw and looked at them.

"It is you who have failed, Odin. The Fateweaver has been used." Algot announced.

Odin trembled in fear, then looked at Loki askance. Loki nodded, and Odin hung his head.

A brooding, expectant silence settled on the three gods as the storm raged all around them. Then, Loki spoke, flames sparking from his tongue. "It is time for the Singularity."

The demiurge then growled. "Bring me Jörð and find that kid." He then glared at Odin, his erstwhile accomplice and ancient enemy. Barking an order to the berserker guards, he then pointed at the old man. They seized him and dragged him from the roof of the tower, while Loki watched without a single word in reaction.

Lan and Linnea arrived at Linnea's house after taking the bus home. Snow fell heavily outside the window as they tried to find words to understand what had just happened.

Just then, Sylvia arrived home, and Linnea asked her, "How was your day?"

Sylvia smiled, "It was really good actually." She then noticed Lan and looked at him suspiciously. "Hey, Lan — how are you? Nice, uh, haircut by the way."

Lan laughed awkwardly and reached up to mess up his hair. "I'm doing much better thank you. How are you, Sylvia?"

"Better, huh? Glad to hear. I'm like, *so great,* actually." Then, to Linnea, she said, "You know what was really weird about this afternoon?"

Linnea laughed briefly. "No, tell me!"

Sylvia did. "For, like, a half hour I found myself ... well, I don't know, praying? Praying quite intensely, to be honest. I can't really explain it, but I just kept thinking about the earth being healed, like this global warming sickness was cured, and that everything would be in balance. I was just praying for the earth and it felt incredible. But it felt like I wasn't alone, you know? Like I was just praying with others, like joining them."

"And since then," Sylvia continued, "multiple things have happened. It is snowing outside for one, and even wilder, the news online is blowing up. People are freaking out. Saying the whole frequency of the earth has shifted. Look at this." She held the phone up so both of them could see the headline.

Worldwide protests call for a "global slowdown."

Linnea looked at Lan with wide eyes. Sylvia continued.

"It's amazing! The stock market has crashed, but everyone is cheering it on. And people are calling for literal revolution and no one is opposing it. Oh, and also, it's not just snowing here, it's snowing everywhere!"

Linnea couldn't believe what she was hearing. She was still feeling the effects of the liquor from Ullr's flask, and everything seemed lined with an animated force. It sounded crazy, maybe, but she couldn't deny a feeling that her life was intertwined with the narrative of the entire earth. And what had their prayer just done?

"I think I need to go see the boys," Lan said suddenly. "I think I owe them an apology. I will come back in a bit. So great to see you, Sylvia!"

Linnea walked outside with him. "Everything okay?" She asked.

"Yeah, sorry, it's been a big couple hours. I really just need to be alone for a second and go for a walk if that's okay. I also have been such a dick to Pierce and Couch Guy recently, I need to go apologize to them."

"Totally understandable!" she said, looking into his eyes. She was so grateful that terrible vibration was gone but she saw something else: the beginning of tears.

"I can't thank you enough, Linnea," Lan said as he hugged her. "For everything."

His arms wrapped around her head and shoulders as she squeezed into his chest. She also felt like she was about to cry, so she did.

"Lan?"

"Yes, Linnea?"

"I think we are wrapped into something much bigger than us."

"Me, too."

"I'm scared."

Lan hugged her tighter. "So am I."

A chthonic cosmic haunted parade of titanic beings marched through the deserted streets of Asgard, bringing a storm with it.

The burning buildings shook to the beat of their drums as Skaði, her staff in hand, led the mass of monstrous beings and manifested her own abominable form. Ullr marched beside her, his antlers reaching into the chaotic sky. The old gods, the Aesir, the Jötunn, and countless others marched behind the two figures.

The new skyscrapers of Asgard crumbled as the vast Jötunn tore them down, corporate giants unable to stand against the much older giants of nature. Trolls and elves and dwarves had all joined the Wild Hunt, eager for the fight against Asgard's usurper. Along with them, eerie shadows also raged: even the draugr in their most horrible forms had joined in this divine revolt.

Ragnarök was beginning. Spring would have to wait.

Despite their numbers and their power, Skaði was worried. She motioned for Ullr to follow her gaze up to the pinnacle of Algot's tower.

"They are all up there. Jörð is up there."

The two gods stared together at the skyscraper and then followed it down to the impossibly high walls of Valhalla. There, at the base of those walls, arrayed in row after countless row, were thousands of Algot's berserkers. The gods and giants would have to make it past those machines to get to Algot.

"Seems simple enough," Ullr said, sarcastically to fight off the despair in the air.

Skaði also felt the despair. She had seen this in her vision, yes. And she knew that Lan's prayer with the Fateweaver would buy them more time — it was after all the only way to shift Algot's plans. But he still had Jörð, and her vision hadn't shown her what could come next.

"We have no choice. We fight for Jörð." Skaði said.

Ullr pulled his bow from behind his back. "Yes, yes we do. But I fight for you, my goddess, my warrior ice queen." He kissed her, and she whispered into his ear something no one else could hear.

Then, Skaði called for the charge.

The monstrous mob set out running towards the army of berserkers with a wild fury. Skaði began chanting. At her words, massive spears of ice ripped from the building's plumbing and plummeted to the ground, piercing through the machine men with ease. The streets heaved as sewers froze and fire hydrants burst with rime, and many of the berserkers lost their purchase on the ground, slipped, and then froze together. Next to Skaði, Ullr let loose arrow after arrow from his bow, piercing multiple berserkers with each shot.

None of the machines could match their divine power, but there were far too many of them. An endless flood of berserkers swarmed in from above the Wild Hunt, and then also from behind, and even the clubs of the trolls barely seemed to dent their numbers.

This will take too long, Skaði thought. *Where are you, Fenrir?*

Lan had wanted to be alone. But, now that he saw the joy in everyone he encountered, he wanted to celebrate with them. *So many people are outside*, Lan thought. He walked down the street, smiling at every stranger he met. As much snow was falling now as it had earlier this winter, and it was piling up fast. People were everywhere, strolling through the wintry streets talking, laughing, and enjoying the snow. Lan even passed someone holding their hands up in the air, their mouth open, just spinning around in circles.

Was I really possessed for almost a whole month? He had wanted to grow up and get his shit together, make some money, make a difference in the world with technology. And now, suddenly, unless he and Linnea were delusional, they had just said a prayer that was changing the world.

All because of this damn thing on my wrist? Lan looked at the armband, the cause of all the trouble. Had it caused trouble, though? Not entirely — it had helped him learn what he really wanted. He was different now because of it. He still wanted to "grow up," but not to make money or even to own land. Instead, he wanted to be connected to everything around him, to care for the world and what was in it. He wanted to find a way to remind people that the Earth is sacred. Maybe he would finally write that book he had always wanted to write — and he would write it about this.

Lan walked past the Naughty Cowgirl parked in the parking lot. He laughed as he looked at it, and then looked up at the apartment building his friends had moved into.

He had hoped Pierce and Couch Guy would be outside since everyone else was, but he walked up the stairs and knocked on the door. No one ever knocked on the door at the Brown House. He then tried to open it, but it was locked.

The door then cracked slightly, and Couch Guy peaked out. "Lan?"

"What's up, bud?" Lan said surprised Couch Guy was being so suspicious.

"Sorry, thought someone was trying to break in when you tried to open the door," Couch Guy said, and then opened the door all the way.

Break in? Lan thought. *That's weird.*

Pierce walked in from his bedroom. "Oh hey. It's you."

"Pierce! Couch Guy! Nice place, guys." Lan paused awkwardly. "Look, I want to say that I am so sorry, guys, I recognize that I have been a real jerk the last few weeks and I don't expect full forgiveness, but I hope we can hang out again at some point soon. You guys are my best friends, and I really miss you. I haven't been myself."

"Jerk?" Couch Guy asked. "No, dude, we actually were just talking about how you finally had your shit together. We realized how much of idiots we have been, partying all the time, having no goals for the future, no real purpose in life."

"You were?" Lan said with surprise.

"Yeah, dude, guess what?" Pierce chimed in, suddenly stoked. "This guy actually came by a bit ago, said he knew you, super charming fellow. He told us he was going to make you rich, told us he was going to make us rich, too. We want you to know that we're fully on board."

"A guy came by that knew me?" Lan was in shock.

"Yeah, he had a flashy business suit, his hair was slicked back, kind of orange hair."

No, thought Lan

"Yeah, he said he was a lawyer," Couch Guy said with a smile, his teeth hardly visible between his bushy beard. "My new hero, actually. Said we could help to distribute this new miracle green technology."

Lan stared at Couch Guy and, with a jolt of fear, he noticed that his bloodshot eyes were quivering. Didn't Linnea say his eyes had done that?

Lan panicked. "Not you guys, too?" He backed away from Couch Guy.

"You okay, Lan?" Pierce asked, moving towards him.

Lan began to head towards the door, but suddenly a knocking came upon it. Couch Guy opened the door, and then, said, "Oh, it's you again!"

Lan's heart pounded as he watched the man walk into the living room. His smile seemed to rage along with his hair like he was made of fire.

"Oh hey, Lan! Funny seeing you here. We missed you this afternoon. Didn't feel like coming to our meeting? Don't want the job anymore?"

Lan looked from the lawyer to Pierce and then to Couch Guy with alarm. He'd walked into a trap.

"You look different, Lan," the man said. "You and the whole world actually, you all seem a bit different. And you must know who I really am, huh?"

Lan gulped. "Loki?"

Loki nodded. "Ah, good boy. Also, that was a cute prayer you said, but it's not exactly the direction we had in mind for things. So, why don't you come with me, Lan? Someone is just dying to talk to you."

"Yeah, Lan," Pierce said, sounding very unlike himself. "Go with him."

Lan's heart sank — he had no other choice. With one last glance at his possessed friends, he followed Loki out of the apartment, down the stairs, and into the parking lot. There, he saw his old landlord, along with his father, both wearing cowboy hats, standing next to the strangest cyber truck he'd ever seen.

"Get in, kid," Loki said, smiling. "You're about to meet God."

Odin walked wordlessly, his steps accompanied by the subtle sound of hydraulics emanating from the berserkers forcing him onward. His guards suddenly stopped and then pushed him into a side corridor to make space for another group escorting a different prisoner to Algot.

Odin saw a flash of green hair between the heads of the guards, and then called out: "Jörð!"

"Odin!" she replied, breathlessly.

"I'm so sorry," Odin said, but she didn't respond.

The prison guards kept walking by, and Odin heard one of them shout in its metallic voice, "Walk faster."

Another voice replied, "I will move at whatever pace suits me."

Odin recognized that voice and then saw the prisoner in a gap of the endless sea of metal. Odin stared at Jörð's new lover, Grandfather, with a twinge of jealousy. The man returned Odin's gaze sternly, but with a look of pity that shook Odin to the core with shame.

More soldiers processed past them, pushing a massive cage. Something ancient and feral was in that cage, gazing out at Odin, with a world-breaking truth.

Odin gazed back and then shook his head in shame. *Despite all we have done,* Odin thought, *the future cannot change.*

Algot had blinded him, confused him, enslaved him. He had enslaved Jörð. And what had this all been really for? Only to numb Odin's fear of death.

"I will die," Odin whispered to himself, finally admitting the one truth he had tried to avoid his entire life.

"I will die," he said again, feeling something strange awaken with him. It was almost funny, this truth. Funny — and relieving.

Odin suddenly laughed aloud. "I will die!" he said, overcome with the release of those words.

Valhalla was once his castle. A place for the warriors who had died. They had died, and then they joined him here. Death had for them also been a release, and also a joy. Yet the god for whom their deaths in battle had been an act of love had been too afraid to admit that he, too, would also need to die.

He laughed again and then remembered something else. All those dead warriors were still here in Valhalla.

Still laughing, Odin then shouted aloud, "I call upon the *einherjar*, you valiant warriors who died in battle and now reside within the walls of Valhalla. Come fight with me one last time, for my Ragnarök has come!"

A cold mist swept through the hallway, accompanied by the distant din of battle. It surrounded them, filling every last bit of space, and then seeped into the guards.

The wailing noise was terrible. Machines that did not know death suddenly felt for the briefest moment what death was. Metallic wails of lament screeched through the halls of Valhalla as the impossibility of machines fearing oblivion suddenly became possible.

All at once, they destroyed themselves in terror.

Odin looked down the hallway at the massacre of automatons and then saw to his dismay that Jörð and Grandfather had already been forced through the door. He then saw the thing he'd feared forever, the fate he'd done everything to escape, play out before him.

The cage had broken, and its prisoner stared at him. Fenrir, the apocalyptic black wolf, Jötunn child of Loki and Angrboða, then miraculously freed himself from the unbreakable bonds.

With blood running down his sides, Fenrir slunk down into a stalk, growled, and prepared to pounce.

Odin nodded. "I will die," he said one last time, and smiled, meeting the fate he'd tried too long to escape.

Algot was tired. His robe was quite dirty, his beard was unkempt, and his hair was tangled and matted. He kept telling himself he would rest. He was going home soon. His endless conquest of the earth seemed to finally be coming to an end. What lay beyond? He could only dream of the heavens.

Loki was far from the only trickster around. He, the demiurge, had not only tricked everyone, he'd even tricked Loki.

He had never intended to stop Ragnarök.

Algot had been planning for aeons, ever since the first moment he found himself trapped on this awful planet. He had needed these petty gods to play along, had needed them to think he could truly change their fate. And they never guessed his real plan: create a technology, powered by their essence, that would allow him to leave this prison forever.

I will be their Ragnarök, Algot mused. He would be their end, merge them into himself, and become a Singular God: the Singularity. Interstellar travel was within his grasp. There was just one final step: Jörð had to die.

Loki suddenly interrupted his thoughts.

"I must remind you, my lord, although dealing with his prayer will be easy, if you kill the young man before he fulfills his Oath to the Fateweaver, you risk destroying it."

Algot scowled at Loki. "You damn trickster, you said it doesn't matter if it's destroyed — the Singularity will still happen."

"Yes, my lord," Loki said with loyal agreement. "But you would be much more powerful with it.

Algot raged, "I would rather the thing be destroyed!" He yelled, shaking his fists. "This goddamned Tree is binding me here."

The sky seemed to mock him, lightning flashing across it. The storm raged all around, and Yggdrasil shook.

Algot tried to calm his voice. "The kid will be sacrificed and the Fateweaver destroyed the moment I become the Singularity. Do you understand?"

Loki smoothed his own voice, making it sound like velvet. "Everything is understood," Loki said, folding his hands in front of him. "Just one final thing."

"What?" Algot boomed.

"You will need to wear the Fateweaver to enact the Singularity," Loki said.

"Fine," Algot boomed, swelling with so much arrogant triumph he missed the slight upward curl of Loki's lips.

Lan opened his eyes slowly. He had no idea where he was. Outside somewhere? He must have fallen asleep when he was with Loki.

Lightning spread across the sky as he realized he was tied up. Moments later, thunder shook the top of the snowy skyscraper as if it had been hit by Thor's hammer. Wind blasted his face, and he was cold.

He looked over to his right and saw someone else was bound beside him, an Indigenous elder who vaguely reminded him of the coyote he kept seeing. The wise man nodded in recognition, and Lan felt a brief moment of comfort.

He then took in more of the chaotic scene, looking over to his left to see that a woman was also tethered, a woman he had seen in vision before. It was Jörð, and her eyes vibrated in the way he'd seen the eyes of Pierce and Couch Guy.

Then he heard a voice.

"Hello, Lan."

Lan turned his head slowly to see an old, hideous man shaking his head at him.

Was this God? Lan wondered. *The angry man I saw in my vision?*

Loki was standing next to the man, smiling. The two figures were accompanied by metallic warriors standing silently in the swirling snow.

The robed man spoke again. "It's time for you to fulfill your true purpose, Lan."

"Huh?" Lan said, groggily.

"The creature of energy that bound you, my digital demon. It possesses Jörð, and she will die unless you bind it to the Fateweaver."

"What?" Lan asked. "I don't understand." He then looked at Loki.

Loki nodded. "It's the only way to save Jörð, Lan. Do what he says."

"No," Lan replied, defiantly. "I'd never trust either of you. I've seen what kind of world you want to build."

Loki shrugged, then nodded to the guards. They then suddenly pulled a woman out from behind their ranks.

It was Linnea.

"Linnea!" Lan flailed uselessly against his bonds. The crazed old man then grabbed Linnea, pulled her up on his lap, and then held a knife to her throat.

"I am Algot, the all-powerful, demiurge of earth, soon to be the ultimate authority of the cosmos, and I command you to do as I say, Ian Winters!"

Lan shuddered and wanted to cry from the terror. But just then, he heard a voice in his head that sounded a lot like his own, saying: *Embrace the trickster.*

Lan looked around him, and then again at Linnea, and suddenly understood.

"Okay," he said. "By the World Tree from which I was made, I bind this digital demon to the Fateweaver."

Algot smiled. "Now, bind the Fateweaver to me."

Lan glanced briefly at Loki, then back at Algot, and did exactly as he was told to do.

Throughout the cosmos, a deep nefarious cackle was all that could be heard. Algot mocked creation as he blasted into the starry sky, leaving his throne, his terrestrial prison, behind. The Fateweaver was now upon his wrist and the digital demon bound to him. His eyes were a blistering white oblivion, and his feet projected him towards his manifest destiny.

He was the only God. The Singularity had come. God and machine had fused together at last.

Loki watched the divine spaceship with joy, awaiting the delicious moment of revelation.

"Loki!" the singular God suddenly screamed, his smile now gone. He had violently bounced back after crashing into an invisible barrier. He then began raging against the intangible wall, trying to fight his way towards the twinkling stars which were still light years away.

"Yes, my lord?" Loki asked, pretending to be curious.

"I do not have all of the power in the cosmos!" He suddenly sounded devastated.

"What do you mean, my lord?"

"I am trying to leave this blasted planet, but for some reason, I cannot! The World Tree still mocks me!"

Loki let the terrified emotional silence of Algot linger, savoring every last bit of it.

"Wait," Algot said slowly. "Why are *you* still here, Loki?"

"Me?" Loki said innocently, floating alongside Algot.

"Jörð is dead, and *all* other gods should have been trapped in the digital prison once I became the Singularity — *including you.*" Algot looked crazier than ever.

"Ah, so you said the quiet part out loud. See, the thing about all this is…" Loki hissed, his fiery tongue forking. "Who was it that gave fire to the humans, Algot?"

Loki was channeling his inner Prometheus, delighting in his nature as Jotunn. "We all know it certainly wasn't you. Also, it wasn't you who showed mankind how to make the net."

Algot looked around himself anxiously, "Where are we?"

Loki shrugged. "You may have tried to control technology, Algot, but it was never actually *yours.*"

"What have you done, Loki? You have ruined everything!"

Suddenly Algot's arm was mysteriously raised by a power beyond him, and the arm ring floated off of it with ease. The Fateweaver hovered in the darkness between the two astral beings, buzzing with an electronic glow.

Loki continued to speak. "You wanted everything accelerated, while everyone else just wanted things to slow down. That was a bit selfish of you, I'd say. But it also looks like you're slowing down, too."

Algot struggled to move, but his limbs had frozen.

Loki raised an eyebrow. "Welcome to the Singularity, Algot, your own personal, singular prison."

Algot's eyes were frozen open.

Loki continued. "Isn't this what you wanted? God and machine united at last?" Loki nudged the floating Algot mockingly.

At that very moment, an electrical wyrm slithered out of the Fateweaver and encircled Algot. The serpent then pulsed around Algot within the digital prison. The Midgard serpent, Loki's child, the digital demon, now bound Algot, the snake from the garden mocking him.

Loki began to laugh now, his whole body lighting up. His shriek echoed throughout the artificial cosmos, as flames danced off his laughter.

The voltaic digital dragon enclosed Algot as an inferno began to rage throughout the strange dimension. Algot's paralyzed body tried to shake in fear; as sweat poured down his forehead and his frayed beard singed. He summoned the last bit of force within him to whisper, voicelessly, to Loki.

"You are Satan himself!"

Loki continued to laugh and then left Algot to his singular hell.

Doubt had become him. Lan had betrayed his oath. He had done what he was told without any agency, and now he hated himself for it. He hadn't returned the arm ring to its owner, he had given it to a thief.

Lan watched Algot rocket into the sky and disappear with a dread beyond words. His whole body was trembling as he heard Jörð cry out in agony. All hope was lost.

But I embraced the trickster!

Just then, a door burst open, and he saw Ullr charge through with vengeance, followed by Skaði, a massive wolf, and a host of other-worldly beings.

Lan watched in disbelief as his bonds came loose. He stood, relief rushed through him, and then he ran to Linnea and hugged her there at the top of Asgard.

Something still unsettled him. Although the world hadn't ended in some terrible instant, Lan couldn't shake that feeling of regret.

"I believe you have an oath to fulfill."

Lan turned to his side to meet the voice. It was Loki, the businessman who had been haunting his every move. Loki was holding the Fateweaver out to Lan, returning it to him.

Lan looked around with fear.

"We don't have to worry about Him anymore," Loki said.

Lan's body was in shock, but he urged it on, knowing it was fully conscious of what needed to be done.

Holding Linnea's hand, Lan approached Jörð and she beamed at him. He handed Jörð the arm ring, and she put it on her wrist. Something that felt like primal love rushed through him as Lan looked at her bulging belly. He then realized that a new worldview was about to be born.

Linnea awoke with sudden concern and reached over for Lan. Her fear subsided as her hand collided with his face. She thanked the gods.

It had all just been a terrifying dream.

"Um, ow." Lan put his hand to his face, and then Linnea's intertwined with it.

"I'm sorry!" she cried. "I just had the scariest dream!"

Lan didn't say anything for a moment as he rubbed his eye.

"That's funny," he finally said. "I was having a crazy dream, too."

He suddenly jumped up into a sitting position.

"It's gone!"

"What's gone?"

"The Fateweaver! The bracelet is gone!"

"That means..."

"*It wasn't a dream,*" they both said in unison, staring at each other in the graceful silence of the dawn.

Lan then whispered: "It's snowing."

Something in the way he said it implied that this fact held a much deeper meaning than usual. Linnea looked outside at the dimly lit flakes and a profound feeling of relief swept through her.

"Do you feel that?" Linnea asked as she noticed a very distinct difference in the energy around her. Everything within the room, the snow outside, the light itself: it all felt so alive.

Lan nodded and smiled, then kissed her before saying, "Come on. Let's go see how much it snowed!"

They walked outside and they were bewildered by the snow's vast beauty. Linnea scooped some of it up in her hands and tasted it. Lan looked at her, laughing, and she offered some of it to him, too.

He ate some, and then she picked up some more, this time throwing it playfully into his face. Lan laughed, licked the snow out of his facial hair with his tongue, and then she kissed him.

They stood there together in that embrace, kissing and then laughing and then kissing again until Linnea's phone buzzed.

They both stopped suddenly and looked at each other with suspicion. Linnea pulled it out of her pocket slowly, and then read the message accompanying the link just texted from an unknown number: "*Massive snowstorms surprise scientists.*"

"Lan? Do you think?"

But Lan didn't reply. Linnea looked at him and then followed his gaze to the edge of the road where a coyote stood looking back at both of them.

52: Jörð Goes Skiing

Jörð hadn't felt this cool since the Pleistocene. The Holocene had been harsh. All of her cycles had been sped up and she had a constant fever. But magically, overnight, her entire worldly body was covered in cool air, and cold, frozen snow.

Oh, joyous snow! How could such a thing not provide so much beauty and bliss and comfort?

Jörð rode along the divine substance now, side by side with Skaði, who looked now so healthy, and Ullr, who looked so glorious. Even Grandfather was there, laughing as he came along slowly on his old but now not-so-tired legs.

Everything now felt so good, and Jörð was skiing pow. Her green hair flowed in the wind as the magical snow shimmied around her.

She held her baby in her arms as she skied, and they giggled and bounced along in the snow, laughing in the healing aura that surrounded them all. She was now finally free, and the powdery white of the Milky Way marked her delighted ski passage throughout the star-filled sky.

ABOUT NATHAN ALEXANDER ROSS

Nathan Alexander Ross is a mystic, snowboarder, photographer, and author. He spends most of his time wandering through the mountains, forests, and rivers of northwest Wyoming. If he is not out in the snow, he is probably flipping through the pages of a book, or scribbling in his journal.

ABOUT SPHINX AND SUL BOOKS

Sphinx is an imprint of Sul Books. Born from a collaboration of two long-time independent esoteric publishers, and named to honor the Suleviae — the sisterhood of goddesses revered at springs throughout Europe — Sul Books is dedicated to publishing works that manifest aspects of the sacred sight that heals what humans have harmed.

As with the thrice-fold kinship of the Suleviae goddesses, Sul Books combines the publishing strength of three resilient imprints: Sphinx Books, RITONA, and Gods&Radicals Press. Arising from these continuing legacies comes a fourth, committed to stand-out works of powerful transformation.

Find our other titles at SULBOOKS.COM